Hard Luck

Also by Frederic Bean
in Thorndike Large Print ®

Hangman's Legacy
Tom Spoon

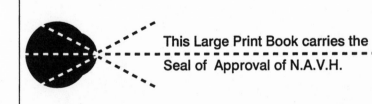

This Large Print Book carries the
Seal of Approval of N.A.V.H.

Hard Luck

Frederic Bean, 1944-

Thorndike Press • Thorndike, Maine

A-1

Published in 1994 by arrangement with Walker Publishing Company, Inc.

All the characters and events portrayed in this work are fictitious.

Thorndike Large Print ® Western Series.

The tree indicium is a trademark of Thorndike Press.

The text of this Large Print edition is unabridged.
Other aspects of the book may vary from the original edition.

Set in 16 pt. News Plantin by Melissa Harvey.

Printed in the United States on acid-free, high opacity paper. ∞

Library of Congress Cataloging in Publication Data

Bean, Frederic, 1944–
    Hard luck / Frederic Bean.
        p.   cm.
    ISBN 1-56054-718-9 (alk. paper : lg. print)
    1. Texas — Fiction. 2. Large type books. I. Title.
[PS3552.E152H37 1994]
813'.54—dc20   93-30999

Hard Luck

Chapter 1

For quite a few weeks now, Dan Willis had known he needed to begin a serious search for a job. Existing on jackrabbits and whatever else he could find along the way, he headed west without a cent to his name, living off the land and rapidly becoming as gaunt in the flanks as his buckskin gelding.

It had been an unusually dry summer, and as fall drew near, the sparse West Texas grasses had all but disappeared. Thus the buckskin horse found precious little to eat as it carried Dan toward his chosen destination, nor had the buckskin's rider fared much better, for even the jackrabbits had departed from this barren stretch of wasteland. And the farther west Dan rode, the worse prospects seemed. He could count the bullets he owned on the fingers of one hand, which made hunting for his supper a serious proposition. A missed shot could mean starvation next week.

Jackrabbits were tricky bastards to shoot,

even when they had ample flesh, and a skinny one was the hardest animal on earth to kill, but Dan was a man without choices. There was nothing else to eat west of the Leon River in the summer of '86, if you didn't count lizards and snakes.

Back home, a place called Possumbelly Flats on the east bank of the Brazos, he'd been given the nickname, "Slim," due to his unusual height and razor-thin frame. At six feet and four, he seldom weighed more than a hundred and fifty pounds fully dressed. Of late, dining on a fare of slender jackrabbits, he'd shrunk to scarecrow proportions; his denims were prone to slide off his hips when he wasn't wearing his gunbelt. The solution had become painfully clear some time back . . . he would be forced to seek employment and earn some money before continuing his travels. As unpleasant as the prospect seemed to a man who hated all forms of labor that could not be performed from the back of a horse, his present circumstances left him desperate. It was work at a menial, humiliating job, or starve.

For weeks he'd stopped off at every ranch he came upon, asking about day work for a cowboy. The drouth had sent cattlemen to the railheads with most of their herds. There was no grass, and cattle were sold off by the thousands: ranches with empty pastures had no work for cowboys. There had been distasteful offers of employment here and there, cutting fence posts in the cedar brakes just west of Waco and chopping firewood for an elderly widow at Lampasas. No greater humiliation could exist than for a cowboy to leave his saddle and carry a woodchopper's axe into a stand of cedars or post oaks to earn his living. It was akin to walking naked down the aisle of church. Rather than face the disgrace, Dan had declined the offers and ridden on, sure of his ultimate vindication farther west. There would be a cowboying job somewhere, and he would still have his pride.

Today, however, he had come to the grudging conclusion that a man's pride could assume less importance in an emergency, which was most certainly the case now. For two days he'd had nothing to eat at all, and when he swung down off the gelding too quickly this morning his head had started to swim. In short order he would be too weak to swing an axe even if he found a woodcutting job and he knew it was time to shed some of his pride. Chopping wood was far better than a slow and painful death from starvation. It was time to act.

As he rode, Dan spoke to the horse. "Swear you'll never tell another soul, Buck, but I'm gonna take the next job that comes my way. Don't matter if it's shovelin' cow manure, I'm gonna take it for a spell and get back on my feet. There ain't enough meat on a jackrabbit in these parts to make 'em worth skinnin' and I'm gettin' a touch weak in the knees." Dan rubbed Buck behind the ears. "You ain't lookin' too awful good yourself lately. Fact is, it's plumb embarrassin' to be seen ridin' a bronc that ain't nothin' but skin and bones. Hadn't wanted to tell you this, ol' hoss, but you're a part of the reason I'll be willing to accept undignified work, such as choppin'. I feel sorry for you, Buck, so I'll be forced to do things I wouldn't naturally, so I can buy you a sack of feed."

The buckskin's ears flipped back and forth.

"You seem mighty damn ungrateful," Dan went on, glancing at the empty hills around him. "If you appreciated the sacrifice I'm about to make on your behalf, looks like you'd hurry as much as you could so I could take the next undignified job we come to. Slow as you've been travelin' the past few days, there's liable to be snow on the ground afore we get to the next ranch. If I wasn't so damn weak just now, I'd get off and walk myself so's I could get there before I die of old age."

The buckskin plodded along at a walk without hastening its stride at all.

Dan gave up talking to the indifferent animal and put his mind on other things. He daydreamed about cutting into a thick, juicy steak that was swimming in its own gravy. He could see it there, floating before his eyes, as the gelding started up a dry caliche hill in a swirl of windblown dust.

Beyond the rise, he saw a group of corrals and a bunkhouse nestled in a stand of live oak trees. "There it is, Buck," he said quietly. "There's the next place we'll call home. I'm gonna do whatever it is they're willing to pay me to do. Don't matter if it's washin' out spittoons, I'm gonna make myself do it plumb till payday. And just so's it won't ruin my reputation, I'll give them another name. Wouldn't want word to spread that Dan Willis is down on his luck."

He roweled the gelding to a trot and reined for the corrals, glancing up at the sun to judge the time. There was a chance that he'd made it in time for the noon meal. If he told the right story to the rancher, he stood a chance of finding some sympathy and a plateful of beans.

"Whatever they've got, it's better'n a rawboned rabbit," he said.

A half mile from the ranch, he noticed more pens and corrals beyond the bunkhouse. "Big outfit," he muttered, although the corrals were empty, and from a distance, the place looked deserted. A cookshack stood beside a windmill near the first corrals. A piece of rusted stovepipe stuck through the roof. "No smoke," he told himself sadly. "If they've got any Pecos strawberries, they'll be cold, but I reckon cold beans are better'n none."

As he rode closer, the place took on a shabbier appearance. Dan's hopes started to decline. "This is damn sure a rundown affair," he said. "Maybe the dry spell put 'em out of business, too. Damn the luck."

He saw a few horses in a corral behind the bunkhouse and a second windmill spinning its wooden blades above the treetops. A sucker rod rattled noisily up and down the windmill's shaft. In a land where water was so scarce, the sound of the windmill was a comfort.

A little cabin stood to the south of the pens, shaded by a grove of live oaks. When the sounds of the buckskin's hoofbeats reached the cabin, a dog began to bark from the porch. Moments later, a cowboy came through the front door to watch Dan ride toward the ranch. Then two more cowboys left the bunkhouse to stare at him, shading their eyes from the sun. One carried a rifle, balancing it in his fist. Dan noticed gunbelts on all three men. Wonder if they've had some kind of trouble, he asked himself.

He reined toward the cabin, ready to tell his story to the ranch foreman, a tale he'd told so many times he needed no rehearsal to remember his lines. Judging by the looks of the place he would need to spin a convincing yarn to wheedle a meal and a job from this outfit. The ranch had a forlorn look about it. If a place could be called neglected, this was it.

The cowboy on the porch gave Dan an unfriendly stare when Dan reined down on the buckskin.

"Howdy," Dan said, putting on his best grin. "Just passin' through on my way to El Paso and thought I'd ask about day work at this here ranch. I'm a dead-shot roper. Catch horns or heels on the first loop every time. I can drag yearlings to a branding fire quicker'n most men can work hot irons. And topping-off bad broncs is one of my specialties. I can ride the worst outlaw you've got and have him ready to pull a buggyfull of women to the church-house on Sunday without spillin' the crock of cream. I've had some hard luck lately, and because of it, I'm willin' to work cheap and go easy on the cookshack vittles. This dun hoss don't eat much either, so I'll be adding an easy keeper to the saddle string, and you can tell the rest of the hands that I don't snore, so I don't bring no disturbance to the bunkhouse at night. I don't gamble or swear very often and I'd rather lose

13

a finger than allow so much as a drop of whiskey to enter my mouth. The name's Dan Smith, and I'll make you a top cowhand, mister. You can take that promise to the bank."

The cowboy's face was blank a moment. Then he shook his head side to side. "I do believe that's the windiest speech I ever heard, Mister Dan Smith. If you're half as good as you say you are, then I'd have to be a fool to let you ride off without a job offer." A wry grin passed over the cowboy's face. "Bein' a smart feller like you claim to be, you know it's a dry year. These pastures are plumb empty right now. I'm a cattle buyer, not a rancher, Mister Smith, and you can see my corrals are empty. But I've got some cattle coming in a few days, and I find I'll be short of pens to hold them until I get them off to the markets. My boys are headed this way right now with a big herd and it just so happens I've got a job for a man who understands building fence."

Dan's face fell. "I never was much with a posthole digger," he said. Digging postholes was even more undignified than cutting posts. Of all forms of labor on earth, the most humbling for a cowboy was working a shovel out in plain sight where everybody else could see him. "I'd rather do most anything else," Dan said. "Pluckin' chickens for the cook, or even

14

cuttin' firewood."

The cowboy shook his head. "Got no chickens to pluck, and the firewood's already chopped. Fencin' is what I'm offering, Mister Smith. Take it or leave it."

A rumbling in Dan's belly brought him closer to a decision. "Just lookin' at this ground, appears it's mighty hard to dig."

"Never said the work was easy," the man replied. "To tell the honest truth, I'm considerin' withdrawing my offer. I swear you look too skinny to dig deep holes, Mister Smith. Don't see how you'd hold up under the strain, thin as you are. Same goes for that dun horse. He's too damn thin to do a day's work, and so are you, in my estimation."

Dan saw fleeting opportunity slipping from his grasp. "I can dig the holes, mister. How much does it pay?"

"Ten dollars a month and food. I'll feed that crowbait horse too, mainly because I feel sorry for him."

Dan let out a sigh of disappointment and swung down from his old, high-backed saddle. For a moment, a reeling dizziness washed through his skull as he steadied himself by holding on to the saddlehorn. "I'll take the job," he said. "Just show me where to hang my gear and point me to the shovels."

The cowboy came down off the porch and

15

extended a handshake. "Jake Logan," he said, sizing up Dan with a careful look. "It's just a guess, but you look hungry. Follow me to the bunkhouse and then I'll see if Cookie has any grub to spare."

"I'd be obliged," Dan replied weakly. He took a few steps behind Logan, worrying that he would fall down before he made it to the cookshack.

"Put that dun in the corral with the others," Jake said. "Then I'll introduce you to a couple of the boys."

The pair of cowboys near the bunkhouse eyed Dan suspiciously when he led the gelding away from the cabin. Dan noticed that all three men seemed edgy. The two watching him were rough-looking types without a trace of friendliness on their faces. When he got to the corral he uncinched the saddle and stripped his gear, then turned the buckskin into the pen, where a stack of hay occupied the other ranch horses. Buck trotted over to the haystack and began to fill his muzzle. Beside the better-fed geldings, Buck made for a sorry sight, all ribs and hipbones and gaunt flanks that made Dan ashamed of himself for using the horse so hard on the ride from Waco.

He met up with Jake at the bunkhouse, feeling the stares of the two cowhands.

"This here's Dan Smith," Jake said, making

a chuckling sound after he said it. "Could be these two gents are some of your distant cousins, Dan. Meet Billy Smith, and Tom Smith. By another odd coincidence, our cook's name is Smith too. Never know'd there was so many Smiths in this part of Texas. Maybe you're all kin?"

Dan shook hands with Tom and Billy. Billy was shorter than Tom, and the gunbelt he wore was a gunfighter's rig, notched low in the front of the holster for a quick pull. Tom was a mean-eyed cowboy with gnarled hands and a surly expression. He merely grunted when he shook Dan's hand, then turned away.

"This way," Jake said. "We'll see what Cookie has that ain't already turned green. We start early around here, Dan, before sunrise. Breakfast an' supper is all you get, so eat good when you get the chance. I ain't runnin' a hotel here."

Dan tossed his war bag beside the cookshack steps and followed Jake inside. Three rough-cut plank tables sat between rows of benches. In a kitchen at the back, big cast-iron cooking pots sat on an old wood stove.

"There's beans," Jake said, peering into one of the pots. "Plates are in the dishpan, an' spoons are in the bucket on the floor. Beans'll be cold, but there's plenty of 'em. Won't be nothin' fancy around here, but it'll help you fill out them denims you're wearing. I swear you're the skinniest feller I ever saw. Maybe Cookie can fatten you up so's you can do a full day's work. Cookie went to town in the wagon to fetch supplies. When you get all the beans you want, I'll show you where I want them holes dug, and mind you, I want 'em deep. First shallow hole I find, you're through. Understand?"

Dan nodded once, his mouth watering at the sight of beans. "I can try to dig 'em plumb to bedrock, bossman, if that's the way you want 'em dug," he said.

Jake laughed. "Won't be deep enough," he replied. "Bedrock's hardly more'n a few inches down, in these parts. You'll have to use a drop bar to bust the rock outa them holes. Now get your belly full, and then come to the house to get the tools."

With a sinking feeling in the pit of his stomach, Dan ladled cold beans onto a tin plate as Jake walked out of the cookshack. Digging postholes in solid rock was man-killing work, and now Dan understood why he'd been hired. Only a crazy man would dig holes in bedrock for a living. Working for Jake Logan promised to be a tough proposition.

He sat on a bench and started shoveling beans into his cheeks as fast as he could without choking. The beans were a tasteless, soggy form of nourishment, but they were far better than stringy jackrabbit meat. Once, Dan glanced at a mirror on the cookshack wall and caught his own reflection. He grimaced when he looked at himself, a week's worth of dark stubble and a flop-brim hat encircled with sweat stains. His faded bib shirt had seen too many washings and mendings. Glancing down, his denims were patched at the knees and his boots were run over at the heels, with holes in the soles that made walking across rocky ground painful. All in all, he presented a sorry sight. Unwashed and unshaven, wearing worn-out clothes, he figured he'd reached the bottom of things just now. Hired to dig holes in solid rock, dressed like a common saddle tramp without a penny to his name, he wondered how he could have allowed himself to sink so low. He most often blamed his plight on hard times, when he thought about it at all, but there were occasions when he wondered. It seemed like hard times had a way of following him wherever he went, like a little black cloud hanging over his head that brought dire circumstances to most any endeavor. Was it just bad luck? What had happened to all his wonderful dreams? Was he jinxed?

He was eating a second plate of beans when he heard boots approaching the shack. Jake came through the door with a dark look on his face. He stopped a few feet from Dan's table.

"One more thing," Jake said. "When you work for me, you don't ask any questions about what goes on around here. When you're in town, you don't talk about things you've seen. You keep your mouth shut and do your job without complaining. If you happen to see things or hear things you don't understand, you go about your business and keep your mouth shut about it. I want that made real clear, Mister Smith. A loose-lipped cowboy ain't welcome around here. Is that understood?"

"Sure is," Dan said quickly, puzzled by Logan's remarks. What was going on at Jake Logan's place that couldn't be talked about?

"Good," Jake grunted. "Now hurry and get your belly full, so I can show you where I want them holes."

Chapter 2

The digging had been even worse than he expected. Barely two inches of caliche topsoil covered beds of solid limestone and a pale blue flint that was like iron. For five of the longest hours of Dan's life, he dug just three postholes before dark. And by the time the sun went down, he was too weak to carry the rock bar and the shovel to the toolshed. A trembling had begun in his arms by midafternoon that made it impossible to hold a dipper of water to his lips without spilling most of the contents down his shirt. Adding to his misery, the two cowboys, Billy and Tom, watched him from the shade of a live oak. When the wagon drove in just before sundown, even the cook took a turn watching Dan dig the impossible holes, grinning through a chin full of gray whiskers while he unloaded barrels and crates from his wagonbed.

At the bunkhouse, Dan found things were little better. His bunk was a thin mattress atop a web of rawhide. Cobwebs and spiders occupied every hidden corner of his bed. When he hung his war bag on a peg above his bunk, he was almost bitten by a scorpion.

He found a small piece of lye soap and took a change of clothes to a pump jack below one windmill, stumbling over rocky ground to wash the dried sweat from his aching body before supper. He had eaten so many cold beans at noon that his stomach had swollen to twice its normal size, but he would not pass up the chance to eat again, smelling the smoke from the stovepipe above the cookshack when he trudged back from the corrals.

All afternoon, he'd wondered about the warning Logan had given him. Why was the bossman worried about what Dan would see here? If Jake Logan was a cattle buyer, as he claimed, then why would he warn Dan to keep his mouth shut about what was going on?

"Don't make much sense," he told himself, peeling off his soiled shirt at the windmill.

He worked the pump jack and finally got water, enough to fill a rusted bucket he found beside the well. Then he took off his gunbelt and coiled it beside his boots. Just four loads remained in the .44/.40 Colt he carried. He owned a Winchester rifle, also a .44 caliber, that was booted below his saddle. More than a few times lately he had almost sold the rifle to buy food for the ride to El Paso. But experienced travelers told him that a good rifle was a valuable tool in the Davis Mountains, where roving bands of Comanches and renegade Apaches still preyed on unsuspecting visitors.

When his denims and longjohns were piled on the ground, he glanced down at his nakedness. It was true: he'd grown thinner in recent weeks. His ribs jutted through his skin, and his legs reminded him of bleached cattle bones. Only his face and hands were sun-darkened. The rest of his body was the color of snow.

"Logan's up to something crooked," he said quietly as he began to apply soap to his skin. "No other reason why he'd say what he did about keeping my mouth shut. There's somethin' about Logan's cattle-buyin' business that ain't square."

He reasoned that Logan was buying stolen cattle from rustlers perhaps. The closest railhead would be at Abilene, a tremendous distance to drive a herd in dry seasons. By Dan's rough guess, the ranch was close to Sonora. At a trading post in Menard, he had been told to stay wide of Sonora unless he considered himself a good shot with the guns he was carrying. Sutton County was said to be an outlaw roost, close enough to the Mexican border that a wanted man could make the ride to the Rio Grande in a couple of days. The old storekeeper had advised steering clear of Sonora if Dan liked his shirt without any extra holes.

So it made sense that Jake Logan could be buying stolen cows from various outlaw gangs . . . unless Logan himself was a cattle thief. The more Dan thought about it, the more worried he became about the predicament he might find himself in if the ranch were a headquarters for cattle rustlers. "Just my luck," he said softly, pouring the contents of the bucket down his chest and arms to get rid of the scant lather, "I wind up diggin' postholes in solid rock for a bunch of hardcases on the dodge from the law."

He dried himself off with a piece of rag he found hanging on a nail in a windmill slat, then donned his clean denims and shirt. "No sense worryin' about it," he told himself, struggling into his boots. "I'm liable to drop dead before sundown tomorrow anyways, what with all that rock to be dug out yonder. If the Lord had meant for this ground to have fence posts, He'd have made it softer in the first place."

He combed through his hair, for no particular reason beyond habit, then socked his hat on his head and started back to the bunkhouse. A cool evening breeze from the south pimpled his skin with gooseflesh. A lantern glowed from a cookshack window, reminding him that supper would soon be ready.

He tossed his soiled clothes on his bunk, wondering where the two cowboys named Billy and Tom might be. It was a good guess that they were already at the cookshack. It promised to be a gloomy meal, after the unfriendly looks the pair gave him earlier in the day.

Before he even entered the cookshack, he smelled frying meat and his mouth began to water. He decided that for a spell he could endure most anything in exchange for a few square meals and ten dollars jingling in his pockets when he finished the month. If he could finish the month without collapsing from sheer exhaustion or going to jail for being caught red-handed with a gang of cow thieves. All things considered, digging holes for outlaws was better than eating jackrabbits and being hungry.

Tom and Billy were seated at one of the tables when he came in. They gave him looks of indifference. The ranch cook looked up from his frying pan atop the stove. He nodded and went back to his cooking without uttering a word or changing his flat expression.

Dan walked over to the table where Tom and Billy sat. "Mind if I join you fellers?" he asked.

Billy shrugged. Tom merely stared at Dan and said nothing at all.

Dan straddled a bench across the table and put on a friendly grin. "That rock's damn sure hard," he said.

Tom scowled. "You're gettin' paid, ain't you?" he snapped, as though Dan's remark irritated the cowboy.

It required no brainpower to conclude that Tom didn't want conversation, thus Dan addressed his next remark to Billy. "What's for supper?" he asked, watching the smaller cowboy's face.

"Meat," Billy replied. He offered nothing more and looked the other way.

Convinced that there would be no pleasantries at the supper table, Dan folded his hands on his lap and watched the cook stir strips of beef in his skillet for several silent minutes more.

"Whereabouts you from?" Billy asked, surprising Dan with the question.

"Possumbelly Flats, north of Waco on the Brazos. Got its name from bein' a poor place to live. Most folks get by on a mess of greens and fried possum. Some claim it's the sorriest land in the state of Texas. Won't grow nothin' but cotton and sunflowers."

Billy shook his head like he understood. "Can't be much sorrier than this place," he said.

Encouraged by Billy's question, Dan looked at both cowboys and asked, "Where did you gents come from?"

Tom's eyes flickered over Dan. "None of your damn business," he said.

Billy nudged Tom's elbow. "My pardner's in a bad mood. Don't pay him no attention. Jake found Tom's bottle of whiskey stashed in the corn crib an' poured it on the ground yesterday. Tom ain't happy about it. Jake said he won't tolerate a drunk cowboy. If you've got any whiskey hidden in your saddlebags, you'd best get rid of it before Jake finds out."

Tom's sullen expression did not change while Billy spoke. Dan hoped to keep the conversation going, perhaps to learn just what it was that Jake Logan didn't want talked about in Sonora. "I never touch the stuff," Dan began. "Time or two, I tried to drink every last drop of whiskey they had in those Waco saloons. Got my skull busted in a fistfight the first time, over a dance-hall whore named Alice. Next time I tried it, I got throwed in jail for fallin' off my horse. Done it right in front of the sheriff's office by pure accident. Got fined six dollars for bein' drunk in public and stayed three days in jail. Worst three days of my whole life, bein' locked in that cell, so I swore off whiskey for good. Once or twice since then I've taken a drop for my nerves, or when I get the cough, but as a general rule I leave it plumb alone. They call it the devil's brew and I'm one man who understands how it got its name. The devil took hold of me both those times in Waco."

Tom aimed a stare Dan's way. "Sounds like the devil's got hold of your tongue, mister," he said. "You've got more wind than a Texas blue norther. If you don't button up that lip, I'm gonna do it for you with a stick of firewood against your skullbone."

Dan bristled. "No call to get so heated up. Your partner asked me a question and I gave him an answer. But while we're on the subject, I wouldn't take kindly to bein' swatted with a piece of wood. I ain't never run from a fight in my life, so if you've still got a hankering to button my lip, we can step outside while our supper's bein' cooked and you can give it a try."

Tom glared at Dan, and Dan glared back. The tension grew heavier.

"I can whip your skinny ass with one hand an' no firewood," Tom growled.

Dan shrugged and got up from the bench. "Suit yourself on it, cowboy." He took off his hat and placed it on the tabletop. "Let's go outside and give it a whirl."

Dan stalked out the door boiling mad, rolling up his sleeves as he went down the steps.

He heard Tom's boots thumping across the wood floor behind him. Halting in a square of lantern light from the cookshack door, he whirled and crouched to wait for Tom.

"The boss ain't gonna like this," Billy warned. He was framed by lantern light as he stood in the doorway.

"This won't take long," Tom said, pitching his hat in the dirt to one side of the steps, then rolling up his sleeves. "I aim to teach this windy bastard a lesson."

Dan lunged forward while the cowboy spoke and swung a right-hand punch at Tom's jaw, before Tom was ready. Dan's fist landed with a sharp crack, jolting him all the way to his shoulder.

Tom's eyes bulged and his knees sagged. He took a step back to catch himself.

Dan swung a left with all his might. The blow caught Tom on his temple, making a resounding thud. Before the punch landed, Dan knew the fight was about to cost him his job, but it had always been Dan's nature to throw caution to the wind where an insult was concerned. And when the left struck, Dan told himself he didn't like the work in the first place. Digging postholes was hardly a job worth keeping anyway.

Tom staggered back against the cookshack wall, then his eyes rolled toward the heavens and he slid down the rough plank boards to the ground, groaning when he landed. The cowboy's arms fell loosely at his sides. His head lolled over on one shoulder, then his eyes shut.

Dan's knuckles were stinging like he'd stuffed his hands into a hornet's nest, but his point was made.

"I'll be damned," Billy said in a quiet voice, staring down at his friend. "Ol' Tom's sure enough asleep. For a skinny feller, Dan, you pack a hell of a wallop."

Dan caught his breath and worked his sore hands. "He asked for it. Said he'd use a club on me."

Billy nodded, still gazing down at Tom. "For a fact, he wanted a fight just now. Reckon he'd take back that remark if he could. He'll wake up after a bit and want his supper. He shoulda known that a feller crazy enough to take a job diggin' rocks would have to be pretty tough." Then Billy looked at Dan. "Maybe you'll make a hand around here after all, Dan Smith. You ain't near as sissified as we figured you was."

Chapter 3

Breakfast was a somber affair. Tom glowered at Dan during the meal, nursing a swollen jaw but saying nothing about the previous night's incident. Billy didn't offer any comments, either, and Dan silently hoped the disagreement would be forgotten. Jake Logan didn't know about the fight, and for the time being, Dan still held a job at the ranch. A job he desperately needed, as miserable as the work was.

They ate fried bacon and biscuits with cups of scalding coffee to wash things down. Tom had some difficulty chewing the meat with a lumpy jaw, a fact Dan noticed from the corner of his eye when Tom's face was aimed down at his plate.

Billy had explained at supper that Logan took his meals at the cabin and never joined the rest of the hands. "He keeps a woman over there," he'd said around a mouthful of beefsteak. Dan had been too interested in the steaks to pay much attention, but this morning he found himself wondering about the woman. There had been no sign of her the day before, and Dan supposed she stayed out of the sun most of the time.

When the meal was finished, Dan pushed up from the bench and carried his plate to the washtub. "Mighty tasty grub," he said to the cook, tossing his utensils into the tub. "Those biscuits were so light I had to hold 'em down so they wouldn't float off my plate, Cookie. Bacon wasn't too salty, the way some of it is, and that coffee was near 'bout as good as my mother's milk."

The whiskered cook glared at Dan. "Save the bullshit for the bossman, cowboy," he said. Then he gave a half-smile and shook his head. "Thanks anyway. Don't get many compliments around here."

Dan left the cookshack in a better mood, having made a start toward friendships with the cook and Billy. He knew better than to turn his back on Tom, not until the soreness left the cowboy's jawbone. Last night's embarrassment would keep Tom on the lookout for an opportunity to square things.

Pale gray dawn brightened the eastern sky as Dan walked past the corrals to the spot where Logan wanted postholes. It would be another pen adjoining the others, roughly a fifty-foot square connected to an alleyway where cattle could be driven to water at a trough below a windmill. Dan's shoulders and arms ached from yesterday's labors, and he knew the going would be harder today. But with a bellyful of food and the promise of a payday at the end of the month, he decided he could endure most anything. He found the bar and the shovel lying where he'd left them and, with a deep sigh, bent down to pick up his tools, facing long hours in blistering heat before his misery would come to an end.

At the next wooden stake where Logan had marked a new hole, Dan began shoveling away caliche topsoil. Three inches down he heard the sickening clank of his shovel blade against rock. He tossed the shovel aside and picked up the iron bar, preparing for the worst part of the job.

A movement in the surrounding trees caught his attention and he halted the motion of the bar. As it was still dark beneath the oaks, he had trouble making out what it was that he saw. At first, he thought it was a loose horse, or a wandering steer that had come to the corrals for water. Then he saw a woman's outline in the shadows below the trees, coming toward him.

He quickly pulled off his hat, remembering his manners. The woman stepped out of the shadows and he could see her clearly.

"Mornin', ma'am," Dan said, giving her a slight bow. "Didn't see you right at first. Lucky thing I wasn't cussing this rock or you'd have heard some ungentlemanly language."

The woman smiled. "You're the new hand, aren't you?" she asked. Her voice was soft and her tone was friendly.

"Yes ma'am, I am," he replied. "The name's Dan. Dan . . . Smith, and I was hired by Mister Logan to build this here fence."

"Jake told me," she said softly, still smiling, suddenly making Dan uncomfortable. She was a beautiful woman, with long auburn hair that hung off her shoulders. She wore a man's blue denims and they fit too tightly around her rounded hips. Her white blouse was open at the neck, revealing the swell of her bosom and just a hint of cleavage. "My name's Jane. Pleased to meet you, Dan Smith." Then she giggled. "Only I reckon Smith isn't your real name, like everyone else around here."

Dan shook his head quickly. "I'm an honest-to-goodness Smith, ma'am, an' that's a fact. Come from a long line of Smiths, I do. There was ol' Charlie Smith, my paw, then there was Elroy Smith who descended from Carl Smith by way of the Mississippi Smiths who gave us our legacy. I'm as blue-blooded as a Smith gets, but I don't figure I'm any kin to Billy or the cook, and I sure as heck ain't no kin to that foul-tempered Tom Smith."

Jane laughed again, and it was a pretty laugh that went nicely with her pretty face. "Nobody uses their real name when they go to work for Jake. It wouldn't be healthy."

"Why's that, ma'am?" Dan asked. Perhaps the woman would tell him the truth about what was going on at this ranch.

She looked him up and down. "You mean you don't know?"

"Not exactly. It has something to do with the cattle, I reckon, but I never was one to stick my nose where it didn't belong. If Mister Logan wants me to know, I figure he'll tell me. But he did say I was supposed to keep my mouth shut about what I saw while I was here."

Jane glanced toward the cabin. Her eyes were a pretty shade of green in the early-morning light. "Then you're not like the others," she said in a quiet voice. "I really shouldn't say any more. The rest of the men will be back at the end of the week and then you'll understand. That was good advice Jake gave you. It wouldn't be a good idea to talk about what's going on out here. If Jake found out you were talking about the cattle . . ."

She didn't finish her remark, making Dan

all the more curious about the cows headed for the ranch. "Just tell me one thing, if you don't mind, ma'am," he began, speaking in a low voice. "Do I need to keep my eyes open for the law while I'm diggin' these holes? Maybe a sheriff's posse? Or the Texas Rangers?"

Jane seemed uncomfortable with the question. "Jake wouldn't like it if he found out I spoke to you. I'd better get back to the house. Jake will be waking up soon. Goodbye, Mister . . . Smith." She was gone before he could think of anything to say.

More puzzled than ever, Dan went back to his digging, dropping the heavy bar into the shallow hole to break the rock. Now he was certain that something crooked was going on at Logan's ranch, and the thought began to trouble him. He figured he had guessed right the first time, that stolen cattle were being driven to the ranch. "Maybe this is where they change the brands," he said to himself. In the toolshed, he had seen all sorts of branding irons and buckets of grease to treat fresh brands. "Next time, I'll look for a running iron," he said, thinking out loud.

He had only seen a running iron once — the day they hanged an outlaw named Ed Dodwell over at Aquila, after a posse found Dodwell's pasture full of cattle with freshly altered brands. The sheriff had shown everyone in attendance at the hanging Dodwell's running iron, which was nothing more than a short iron rod with a long handle. The short rod, when it was heated, could be used to change a Bar to a triangle or a box on a cow's flank, or alter most any letter in the alphabet so it was hard to read. A brand was proof of ownership, and if the brand couldn't be read, the cow's ownership was in doubt. The running iron was all the evidence the sheriff needed to put the noose around Dodwell's neck and let him swing. Thus Dan concluded that if Jake Logan had a running iron on the place, he was up to no good with the cattle his men were bringing to the ranch. It made sense, after the warning Logan gave him.

"Wonder if I'll make it to payday?" Dan grumbled, slamming the bar into the hole with extra force. "And if the law shows up, they'll figure I'm in on it too. I'll wind up in jail for digging postholes around stolen cows."

He continued his deliberations through midmorning, until his thoughts drifted to the woman named Jane. She didn't seem to fit with an outlaw gang, and Dan found himself wondering about her. It was easy to see that she was Logan's woman, for she slept in the house with him.

"She's damn sure a pretty little thing," Dan

whispered, allowing himself a grin when he remembered her.

As the day wore on, Dan spent more time watching the hills around the ranch while he dropped the bar into the holes. He worried that a posse might come riding in, or a handful of tough Texas Rangers. Would a lawman believe that he had only signed on with this outfit the day before? To dig postholes?

At noon he went to a windmill trough, where he cupped water over his sweating face and drank a dipper of water. His arms and shoulders ached and his knees had a trembling weakness in them that threatened to shake his denims off his hips. He had gone to work without his gunbelt, not wanting any added weight, but now he found himself wishing for his gun. Just in case a posse showed up and started shooting before he was given a chance to explain what he was doing here.

He returned to his digging, now and then glancing toward the cabin, wondering about Jane. Good-looking women were a rare find away from larger towns, in Dan's experience. Was she Logan's wife? She wasn't wearing a wedding ring to declare that she was another man's property.

By the middle of the afternoon, he'd grown so weak that he could barely lift the bar to break rock. "Damn thing got heavier since this morning," he complained bitterly.

There had been no sign of Billy or Tom or the cook, nor had Logan left the cabin all day. It was as though Dan were alone on the ranch, and it seemed curious that no one else was about. He wondered idly if the others were watching him from a window in secret as he tried to keep his pants from falling down, having a good laugh about it. Or was something else afoot that kept the others inside? It was only guesswork, to try to figure things out.

Summoning what strength he had left, he went back to work on the sixth hole of the day, banging the point of the bar against a layer of limestone. Shaking with fatigue, he cursed the fates that had brought him to the Logan ranch and the seemingly unending string of misfortunes he had suffered since he started west. It had all started as idle banter, the idea to ride for El Paso, and beyond. If only he hadn't been listening to that drummer.

A traveling peddler claimed that lands to the west of El Paso offered opportunity for a man who could swing a rope. Big cow spreads in the New Mexico Territory were begging for experienced cowhands, the drummer insisted. Wages for cowboys went as high as thirty dollars a month, and it was all open, unfenced land where a free-spirited man could enjoy peace and quiet. It had all sounded like the perfect place for Dan Willis, back then. A cowboy's life on the open range, drawing thirty dollars a month for doing a job he liked. There had only been one miscalculation when he left to seek his fortune . . . his pockets were empty. The little bit of food he had was soon gone, and there was no day work for a cowhand to be had along the way. It was the dry year, he knew, that brought him to the brink of starvation. It was fate that kept rain clouds from the skies above Dan's travels, the same dark fate that seemed to follow him wherever he went these days.

When exhaustion forced him to rest, he noticed the spotted dog was watching him. The big black and white cur had come to the closest patch of shade to witness the digging. Since no one was about who might eavesdrop on the one-sided conversation, Dan put the bar down and spoke to the dog.

"C'mon over, Spot," he said. Then he whistled.

The dog growled and showed its teeth.

"Take it easy, Spot. Ol' Dan ain't gonna hurt you." He whistled again and patted his pants leg. He had always fancied himself as having a special way with animals and he was sure he could win the dog over, given time.

The dog growled again and refused to

budge, so Dan took a step toward the tree where the dog was lying. The growling grew louder and the dog bared its teeth.

"Easy, boy," Dan whispered, advancing carefully. "I'm your friend."

With lightning suddenness the dog charged him, snarling and snapping its jaws. Dan tried to sidestep the attack, but he was much too slow. Gleaming white teeth fastened on Dan's pants leg and there was a sharp tearing sound. Dan aimed a kick at the dog and almost lost his footing. A hunk of faded denim tore away in the dog's jaws, then the dog ran off with the piece of cloth dangling from its mouth, trotting back toward the cabin porch.

"Ill-tempered bastard ruined my britches," Dan muttered, as the dog reached the porch with the section of Dan's pants. "I do believe this is about the unfriendliest place I ever saw. If I had to take a guess, I'd bet that's Tom's dog, judgin' by its disposition."

He was distracted by the sounds of a running horse from the north. On a barren hilltop, he saw a swirl of dust, then a fast-moving rider headed for the ranch.

"Wonder what's got that feller in such an all-fired hurry?" he asked aloud, squinting at the hilltop.

The horseman raced a lathered sorrel off the hill and into the trees around the ranch, kicking up a billowing dust cloud in his wake. Dan watched the rider spur for the cabin, oddly slumped over his horse's withers. Less than a hundred yards from the cabin, the cowboy slipped sideways and tumbled from his saddle. Landing disjointedly, arms and legs askew, the man slid to a halt near the base of a live oak and went still.

"That feller's hurt bad," Dan exclaimed. He took off in a run for the tree. The sorrel galloped to one of the corrals and made a sliding stop at the fence, but Dan's attention was on the fallen cowboy. Even before he got near the tree, he could see blood on the front of the cowboy's shirt.

When he knelt down, he found the man unconscious. A dark bullet hole in the cowboy's chest sent a trickle of blood down his ribs. The wounded man would have to have a doctor. Dan looked around the ranch and started yelling for someone to come out and help him carry the injured cowboy to the house. By the amount of dried blood on the cowboy's shirt, Dan was certain time was running short.

Chapter 4

No one answered Dan's cries for help. He got up, puzzled by the silence, and hurried toward the cookshack, where he expected to find the cook. The injured man would have to be loaded in the wagon for the trip to the closest doctor. As Dan trotted past the corrals, he wondered why no one heard his yells. Where was Logan? And Billy and Tom? Where the hell had everybody gone?

He found the cookshack empty. Outside, he looked toward the horse corral, where his buckskin and the others were kept. Only then did he notice that some of the ranch geldings were missing, and the top rail of the corral fence had empty spots where saddles were usually kept.

"Where'd everybody go?" he cried. A glance toward the cabin revealed nothing. Logan was nowhere in sight, nor was there anyone else to help him with the wounded cowboy.

"I'll have to harness a team and haul him to town myself," Dan muttered.

Then he remembered the woman. Jane would know something about dressing wounds and caring for the sick. Dan wheeled for the cabin and ran as fast as his feet would carry him to the porch.

A low growl reminded Dan about the dog. "Hey, lady!" he cried. "Hey there, Miss Jane! Come outside, ma'am. A man's hurt!"

Out of breath from his run to the cabin, he kept a wary eye on the dog, listening for sounds behind the cabin door. Where was the woman, he wondered? A man was bleeding to death and nobody seemed to notice. Where the hell was Logan?

He heard the door open. Jane's face appeared through the crack in the door.

"A man's been shot!" Dan exclaimed, still gasping for breath. "He's bleedin' mighty bad."

Jane opened the door and came out on the porch, looking in the direction Dan was pointing. "I'll get some bandages," she whispered. "Who is he?"

"Can't rightly say, ma'am," Dan replied quickly. "I figured he must work for Jake, the way he came ridin' up to the place."

Suddenly Jane looked toward the barn, then toward the bunkhouse. "Where are the others?" she asked softly, and it seemed to Dan that her face was pinched with worry.

"Everybody's gone, including the cook," he replied. "I was yellin' my head off, till I saw that saddles and horses were gone."

"I'll fix bandages," she said, heading for the door.

Dan started back toward the live oak tree, puzzled by Jane's reaction, the worry he saw on her face. He was sure that it had to do with the rest of the men and not the man with the bullet in him.

Dan knelt beside the unconscious cowboy. A pool of blood had grown around the man's chest. His ribs rose and fell, but only slightly. "He's near 'bout gone," Dan whispered to himself.

Moments later, he heard footsteps. Jane came running toward the tree with strips of bedsheet and a tiny glass bottle. She seemed to be looking at the surrounding hills as though she expected someone.

When Jane reached the cowboy, Dan saw recognition on her face.

"That's Bob Huffman," she said, kneeling down. Her gaze fell to the bullet hole. "It's bad," she added, as her fingers went to work unbuttoning the cowboy's shirt.

Dan frowned. "Does this feller work for Jake?"

Jane nodded, opening the bottle, then poured a strong-smelling oil into the wound. She glanced up at Dan with a nervous look. "Jake sent Bob up north a few days ago, to see about . . ." She did not finish her remark, puzzling Dan all the more.

"He's lost a lot of blood," Dan said needlessly. "He needs a doctor real bad. I'll go hitch up Cookie's wagon and drive him to Sonora. There'll be a doctor there."

While she was applying a bandage, the cowboy stirred. His eyes batted open. For a time, he stared blankly at the sky, then his gaze wandered to Jane and he blinked, trying to focus. "Tell . . . Logan. Cade . . . double-crossed us," he croaked hoarsely. A sharp stab of pain made him wince, then his eyes closed.

"Who's Cade?" Dan asked, standing up to go for the wagon.

Jane wouldn't look at him when she answered. "A man who used to work for Jake."

All at once, the cowboy stiffened, arching his spine. A groan whispered from his lips and his bootheels dug into the caliche where he lay. The muscles in his arms and legs started to tremble.

"Bob won't last long enough to get him to town," Jane said in a quiet voice. "No sense harnessing the team, Dan. It'll be over soon."

Dan hooked his thumbs in his front pockets.

46

"Don't hardly seem right not to make the try," he said. "Them postholes can wait."

Jane looked up at him. "You haven't seen very many men die before, have you?" she asked.

Dan shrugged and shook his head. "Not too awful many, I don't reckon," he replied. "Seen some die from natural causes. Saw a man hung once."

Jane nodded her head. "When they start shaking like this, they don't last much longer," she whispered. "But if you want to hitch up the team, I won't stop you."

Dan was torn. The man lying at his feet needed help. It seemed odd that Jane did not agree. "It would be the right thing to do," Dan said quietly. "If you've got no objections, I'll go fetch the wagon." Then a question popped into Dan's head. "What did he mean when he said Cade double-crossed Logan?"

Jane fixed him with a look. "You'd better mind your own business around this ranch, Dan."

"There's somethin' strange goin' on around here, ma'am, and if I'm gonna work here, I'd sure like to know what it is."

The cowboy's arms and legs relaxed. Now his breathing was shallow, irregular. Jane looked down at the cowboy, then back to Dan. "If I were you, I'd saddle my horse and ride out of here before Jake and the others get back," she said softly. "You seem like a nice fellow. You don't belong here."

It struck Dan, while she was talking, how lovely she was. "If there's anything goin' on that's against the law, then you don't belong here either," he said. "Nice lady like you, it don't figure that you're a part of anything illegal."

She smiled at him, and her smile touched something in the pit of his stomach. "That's about the sweetest thing anyone has said to me in a long time, Dan. But I'm Jake Logan's wife. I'm stuck here. Now why don't you run along and harness that team."

Dan turned on his heel, then hesitated and looked over his shoulder. "It surely ain't none of my affair, ma'am, but there ain't no reason good enough for a woman like you to be involved in something dishonest, if it goes against your grain."

Jane wiped the cowboy's brow. "It's not something I can change now," she whispered, and Dan would have sworn that a tear came to her eyes. "Run along now, and get that wagon if you've a mind to."

Dan's head was filled with more questions as he trotted for the barn and corrals. What did Jane mean when she said it wasn't hers to change now? Was Jake forcing her to be a part of some crooked scheme? She said she was Jake's wife, answering one of Dan's first questions about her. But was she a prisoner here? Would she leave the ranch if she could?

He raced around the barn, gathering harness, then out to the corrals to catch the team of mules, all the while asking himself a whole hatful of questions about Jane and her involvement in whatever might be going on at the ranch. When the mules were harnessed to the wagon tongue, he jumped to the seat and slapped the reins over the rumps of the mules, hurrying toward the tree where Jane knelt over the cowboy.

When Dan reached Jane's side, he did not like the look on Huffman's face. All the color had drained from the cowboy's cheeks, and his breathing was so shallow that it was almost impossible to see.

"He's fading fast, Dan," Jane said, watching the cowboy's face. She looked up and pointed to a pair of wagon ruts leading north. "That's the road to Sonora. It'll take you four or five hours in that wagon. We can pile some blankets in the back, so the ride will be softer." She looked at Dan. "I don't think Bob will make it, but you can try."

She got up and trotted for the house while Dan lowered the tailgate on the wagon. Jane came running back with an armload of quilts.

As she came toward the wagon, she cast a look at the trees and the hills around the ranch, and Dan recognized the same worried look he had seen on her face before.

They piled the quilts in the wagonbed, near the back. Dan bent down and lifted the cowboy into the wagon. His arms hung loosely when Dan hoisted him to the makeshift bed, and he groaned when Dan placed him gently on the pile of quilts.

"Tell the bossman I'll be back quick as I can," Dan said, closing the tailgate quickly. He turned to Jane. "I'll think about what you said," he added. "About pulling out. I sure needed this job, but I ain't lookin' for any entanglements with the law."

When Jane said nothing, Dan started for the front of the wagon until he heard her voice behind him.

"Don't say anything to Jake . . . about what I said. Don't tell him you talked to me."

Dan paused at the front wagon wheel and looked at her. "I won't mention the part about clearing out," he said.

Jane shook her head. "You don't understand, Dan. Don't tell him you talked to me at all." She lowered her eyes briefly. "I'm not supposed to talk to *any* of the hands. It'll go hard for both of us if he finds out we talked while he was gone."

It was then that Dan noticed a purple bruise on Jane's left cheek, although she'd tried to cover it with a spot of rouge. He stared at the bruise a moment longer. "He'll hit you, won't he," Dan said quietly. "That's how you got that mark on your face."

Jane shook her head silently, then turned for the cabin; this time Dan was sure he saw tears in the corners of her eyes. "You'd better go now," she said. "Jake might show up, and then we'd both have to explain."

A string of words tumbled from Dan's mouth before he had time to think. "A man hadn't oughta treat a woman like that," he said.

Jane stopped a few yards away. She didn't look at Dan when she spoke. "I'm making my own plans, for when the right chance comes along." Then he saw her finger a tear from her cheek. "You be careful around Jake," she said in a voice that was almost a whisper. "You don't know him. He might get mad enough to kill you if he found out you've been talking to me." She sniffled back more tears. "There was this young cowboy last year . . . he came to the house with some pretty flowers he picked for me. It was springtime, and they were such beautiful flowers. Jake rode up and saw the flowers. He didn't even ask why the boy had picked them, he just . . ." Suddenly

51

Jane buried her face in her hands, then slowly drew her palms away and dried her cheeks with the back of her hand. "Get away from this place, Dan," she said. "Don't get involved in what's happening here. When the opportunity comes, I'm getting as far from this ranch as I can and you'd better do the same. And don't bother talking to the sheriff in Sonora about any of this. He's a friend of Jake's. He takes money from Jake to look the other way."

The look on Jane's face had changed while she spoke. In place of the fear Dan had seen before, there was a determined expression. An edge had crept into her voice, leaving Dan without a doubt that she had made up her mind to go.

Chapter 5

The wagon rattled over a bald prairie, moving steadily north as Jane had directed. Sonora was four or five hours away across rough country and it would be dark before Dan got the injured man to town. As the wagon jolted and creaked along the faint ruts, he thought about his predicament. Quite by accident he had stumbled upon some sort of illegal operation, he was sure of that. And to make matters worse, there was Jane. Dan was more certain than ever that she was being held against her will at the ranch. The bruise on her face was proof enough that Jake was cruel to her. And hadn't she said something about making her own plans? Were they plans to bring the Texas Rangers down on Jake's operation? Or merely to escape?

"It ain't really none of my affair," he told himself, listening to the rattle of the wagon, but his voice lacked conviction. Dan felt sympathy for the woman's plight. "She could just pack up and leave when Logan ain't around," he said. "Unless maybe she figures he'll come after her. She said he was the jealous type."

The story Jane told about the young cowboy who brought her the flowers hung heavily in Dan's mind. She hadn't finished the story, and he couldn't help but wonder what Logan had done to the boy.

"She's a pretty lady," Dan said aloud, after a half mile of silent contemplation. "But I'd be a fool to stick my nose where it isn't wanted. She didn't ask me to help her, but I would. If she asked. A man's got no right to hit a woman, not for the best reason there is. If she asked me, I'd help her get away from that ranch."

Later, after turning around for a look at Bob Huffman, Dan sat with his eyes glued to the horizon while the mules trotted along the wagon ruts. "If I had any sense," he said softly, "I'd pack my gear and head for El Paso, then up to the New Mexico Territory. I'd forget about Jane Logan and whatever it is they're doing at the ranch. I got my own plans to think about, and I'm liable to wind up in jail if I hang around a place where there's stolen cattle. If the law shows up, they'll haul me to jail just like the others."

But the farther north he drove the wagon, the more he thought about Jane, remembering

54

the tears she'd shed, and the fear he saw in her eyes when she talked about Jake. "She's plain scared," he said. "She needs my help. So there it is, Willis. You can't just saddle up and ride off. That woman is a prisoner there, an' your conscience ain't gonna let you ignore it. A man with any principles at all would offer his help to the lady. I could take her with me as far as El Paso, makin' sure she's safe. I'll be stickin' my tail in a crack over it, but that's damn sure what a man with any principles oughta do."

Thus, like a moth drawn to a candle, Dan came closer to a decision to help the woman escape . . . if she wanted his help at all.

Sonora was a collection of clapboard shacks and false-fronted stores along a single dusty street. Dan first saw the town as he hurried the wagon over a rise. Lantern-lit windows cast pale yellow shadows across the road through town as Dan slapped the reins over the mules' rumps to force them into a run. A few horses stood hipshot in front of a saloon at the middle of town. Dan heard someone banging a piano inside, playing a slightly off-key melody.

Dan saw a cowboy rolling a smoke in front of the saloon as he slowed the wagon. He hauled back on the reins to halt the team and waited for the dust to settle.

"Where's the doctor's office?" he asked.

The cowboy shook his head. "We ain't got one. Got us a dentist who knows how to treat the croup and some other things, but Sands is liable to be too drunk to do much of anything about now. If it can wait till morning, you'll be better off. Don't appear to me that you're very sick, stranger."

"It's the feller in the back of the wagon," Dan explained. "Got a bullet hole in his chest. Don't figure he'll live to see another sunrise unless he gets some doctorin' real soon."

The cowboy pointed to the end of the road. "Down yonder. Last house. You'll see the sign."

"Much obliged," Dan answered, shaking the reins over the team. He drove down the street, past a sign above the sheriff's office, remembering what Jane said . . . that the sheriff worked for Jake Logan. At the edge of town he found the dentist's house, and a light burning in one of the windows.

He jumped down from the wagon seat and hurried up the front steps to knock. A muffled voice answered his knock, then there was the scrape of a chair and heavy footsteps.

A paunchy, balding man opened the door to peer out into the darkness. "It's late," he said. Dan could smell the whiskey on his breath.

"Got a feller hurt bad in the back of this wagon. Took a bullet in his chest," Dan explained.

"I'm a dentist, son," the old man replied. He was weaving as he tried to keep his balance in the doorway.

"He'll die without some doctorin'," Dan went on, pointing to the wagon.

The dentist let out an impatient sigh. "Bring him in. Put him in that dentist's chair in the front room. I'll do what I can for him."

Dan carried the limp cowboy up the porch steps. In the dark he couldn't be sure the man was still breathing. A lantern was lit on a table beside a chair with foot pedestals and a head rest. Dan lowered the unconscious cowboy into the chair.

Dr. Sands put on his spectacles and looked down at the man's face, supporting himself against the back of the chair. Then he fingered away the bandage covering the cowboy's wound, scowling. For a time, the dentist was silent, lifting the cowboy's eyelid and then opening his mouth.

"Can't do a thing fer this owlhoot," Dr. Sands said.

Dan frowned. "Can't you do anything at all?"

The dentist shook his head side to side.

"He'll die if he loses any more blood," Dan protested.

The dentist shook his head again. "This one won't bleed any more, son. He's already dead. Now get him outside, before he starts to stink. Hot as it is, he'll start smellin' bad in an hour or two and I can't have him smellin' up my office. Homer Daniels does some undertaking on the side. You can haul your friend over to Homer's and he'll build you a box."

Dan pulled off his hat to sleeve the sweat from his forehead. The drive to Sonora in the wagon had been too long for the cowboy. "He ain't my friend, Doc," Dan said. "Don't even know very much about him. He came ridin' in at Jake Logan's place this afternoon with that bullet hole in him. I was told he worked for Logan."

The dentist stared at Dan for a silent moment. "Are you . . . one of them?" he asked.

Dan wasn't sure how to answer the question. "I signed on at Logan's place yesterday to dig postholes. Can't say as I'd be called a regular hand."

Dr. Sands nodded. "Forget that I asked, son. Now get this body out of here. Place smells bad enough the way it is."

Dan lifted the cowboy and carried him out on the porch. A pale silver moon showed him the way to the back of the wagon. He heard the door slam behind him as he placed the body atop the pile of blankets. "Reckon you took your last ride, stranger," he said, fastening the tailgate. "Wonder if it was that Cade who shot you? Wish you'd had time to explain . . ."

As Dan went back to the wagon seat he remembered the dead cowboy's final words: *Tell Jake. Cade double-crossed us.* "Wonder just what the hell that means?"

He swung the team around and started back through town, giving thought to stopping off at one of the saloons to ask some questions about Logan and what was going on at the ranch. It would be a risky undertaking, should he ask the wrong man in a strange town. Word might get back to the Sonora sheriff that someone was nosing around in Jake Logan's affairs.

"I need some answers," he said, passing the row of brightly lit saloons. The piano music he heard before had stopped. The town was quiet, except for the rattling of Dan's wagon as he drove along the street. "Maybe the undertaker will tell me what I want to know."

He watched for the undertaker's sign atop the false fronts of buildings, wondering if he should take the dead man's body back to the ranch or leave it with the undertaker. He had no authorization from Logan to buy a coffin. "Maybe the cowboy has some money in his pockets, so he can pay for his own funeral."

Passing a side street, he saw a blacksmith's

shop, and a sign that read, "Homer Daniels." The place was dark, but there was a shack behind the building with a light burning behind one window. Dan swung the team and drove up in front of the blacksmith's shop.

At the back of the wagon he lowered the tailgate and stuck a hand in the dead man's pockets. He found a handful of coins. By the light of the moon he counted nine silver dollars and some small change. "Wonder if that'll bury a man?" he asked.

He walked back to the shack and knocked on the thin plank door.

"Who's there?" a deep voice growled.

"Dan Smith. Got a man out here who needs an undertaker."

Boots scuffed across the floor, then the door opened. A burly giant peered out at Dan, blinking to see in the dark. "Where's the body?" he asked gruffly. "I was fixin' to go to bed."

"Out front, in the wagon," Dan replied.

"Who is he?"

Dan shrugged. "Just a cowhand. He rode up to the Logan ranch with a bullet in him. He was dead by the time I got to town."

Daniels made a face. "Don't surprise me none," he said. "I get six dollars fer the box, an' a dollar to dig the hole. Did Logan send any money?"

Dan shook his head. "Jake don't know about it yet. But whoever the cowboy was, he had enough money in his pocket to bury him. Show me where you want him unloaded and I'll hand you the price."

"Logan's bunch," Daniels grumbled, starting around Dan to step off the porch. "There's liable to be a whole lot more dead men around here on account of Logan."

Dan followed the blacksmith to the wagon, figuring a way to ask questions without making Daniels suspicious. "I've been away from the ranch for a spell," Dan began, dropping the tailgate as he spoke. "Has there been much trouble out at Logan's?"

"Some," Daniels said. "Always is when you get a bunch of gunslicks in the same place. You grab this feller's feet and I can get his arms. Ain't been dead long, this one ain't. Not stiff yet. Never saw this gent before. Some of 'em come to town now and then, to buy a little whiskey. Come to think of it, I ain't never seen you before, either."

"Like I said, I been gone for a spell," Dan answered quickly, lifting the dead man's boots. "Just wondered if there'd been any trouble while I was away."

Daniels swung the body off the wagonbed. "I make it a habit to mind my own business when it comes to that ranch," he said. "Most everybody knows what's going on out there, but folks with any sense keep out of it. If you ain't careful, mister, you'll wind up just like this gent, workin' for Jake Logan. It ain't the safest job in Sutton County."

It was three o'clock in the morning by the time Dan drove the wagon down to the ranch. Homer Daniels hadn't told him much that he didn't already know. On the drive back to Logan's, Dan gave serious consideration to pulling out at sunrise. If it hadn't been for the woman, the choice would have been easy, for it was plain that Jake Logan spelled trouble. Dan knew he could wind up doing a stretch in prison if he stayed any longer. But he couldn't ignore what Logan was doing to Jane.

A light was burning in the cabin as the wagon rolled toward the corrals. Before Dan could get the team stopped at the cookshack, he saw Jake come out on the porch carrying a lantern. Dan swung down from the wagon seat and started unfastening the mules.

"Tell me what happened," Jake said, when he reached the wagon.

"The cowboy was dead by the time I got to Sonora," Dan replied, wondering how Jake would take the news.

"Did he say what happened? Who shot

him?" Jake asked.

"Never had very much time to talk, but he was mumblin' something about a gent named Cade."

"Amos." Jake sighed. Then he looked Dan straight in the eye. "Did he say anything else?"

Dan shrugged, wondering how much he should tell. "Said this Cade double-crossed somebody. Said to tell you about it. Seein' as I didn't know what he was talking about, I didn't pay much attention. I was busy tryin' to get this wagon hitched and get him to a doctor. What he said didn't make much sense to me."

Jake nodded. "You've had a long drive, Dan," he said. "Get some shuteye." He turned away from the wagon, then stopped and looked over his shoulder. "Was there anybody else around when Bob rode up?"

Dan shook his head. "I was all by my lonesome. Billy and Tom and the cook were off someplace else. Had to hitch this team and load that cowboy by myself."

"The others were with me," Jake replied. "I was just wondering . . . did a woman come out of the house while I was gone?"

Dan's mouth went dry when he heard the question. "No, sir, I sure didn't see no woman. I'd have remembered it, if there was one. Have you got yourself a wife in there?"

Jake turned on his heel without answering and walked toward the cabin. Dan held his breath a moment, then lowered the wagon tongue and led the team to the corrals.

When he entered the bunkhouse, someone stirred, then a match was struck to a candle. Billy was sitting on his bunk in his longjohns.

"What happened to Bob Huffman?" Billy asked.

Dan pulled off his hat and hung it on a peg. "If that's the feller with the bullet in him, he's dead."

Billy nodded once. "I saw the blood on the ground where he fell off his horse. Another thing I saw was the woman's footprints at the same place. Jake, he was madder'n hell when he saw that the woman had been outside. Jake said he aimed to ask you about it, if his woman came out to help you with Bob."

Dan swallowed. Logan had known all along that Jane had come out of the cabin to help with the injured man. "I didn't see a woman," Dan lied. "Maybe she came out to see what was going on while I was harnessing the team."

Billy grunted and snuffed out the candle. "Jake'll teach her a lesson," he said, stretching out on his bunk. "Jake don't tolerate no foolishness when it comes to women. A word of advice, Dan — if you happen to see a woman around that house, stay clear of her. She's Jake's woman and he'll kill any man who gets too close. I figured you oughta know, so you wouldn't make a dumb mistake and get Jake mad."

Just before Dan dropped off to sleep, he thought about Billy's remark. Had Jake Logan killed the young cowboy who brought the flowers to his wife? Did that explain why Jane ended the story before she finished telling him what had happened?

Chapter 6

He was late for breakfast. Billy and Tom were saddling horses when Dan left the bunkhouse and there was no smoke from the cookshack stovepipe. Cookie scowled at him when he came in.

"Food's cold," Cookie said.

"I got back late," Dan replied, taking a plate of cold biscuits and bacon. "That cowboy was already dead by the time I got him to Sonora. Did the best I could for him, but it was too late."

Cookie nodded and took off his greasy apron. "You shoulda left him where you found him. Nobody liked Bob much anyways. This ain't no place for softhearted gents. If it had been Bob who found you with a bullet in your guts, he'd have emptied your pockets and left you for dead."

The subject of money reminded Dan of the silver dollars and sixty cents belonging to the dead man. The coins were nestled in Dan's pocket. "I couldn't just walk off from a man who was bad hurt," Dan answered, biting into a biscuit. "It goes against my grain."

Cookie grunted. "Won't win you any favor with Jake," he said. "Jake's a hard hombre. Tough as bootleather. When a man hires on with this outfit, he'd better be the same. Jake won't tolerate a tenderfoot. If you stay on, you'll learn to mind your own business and do what you're told. And there's one more thing . . . stay away from the house. Jake's woman lives there, and unless you want to tangle with Jake, you'll stay clear of the house."

"A woman?" Dan asked, trying to sound surprised.

Cookie gave Dan a look. "Calls her his wife. Stay clear of her, or you're liable to have some serious regrets. Jake don't allow her to talk with the rest of the hands. She stays inside most of the time."

"Didn't figure the bossman for jealous."

The cook shook his head, busy with scrubbing a cast-iron skillet and not looking at Dan. "Worst I ever saw when it comes to his womenfolk," he said quietly. "Don't try to talk to her if you see her around the place." Then Cookie gave Dan a sideways glance. "One time, she tried to run off and leave him. He followed her plumb to Abilene. Busted up

her face somethin' awful when he found her."
Cookie frowned. "Then there was this other
time, when Jake figured she was plannin' to
run off with a new hand." The cook grunted
and wagged his head. "Jake fixed the both
of 'em that time."

"So what happened to that new hand?" Dan
asked in a matter-of-fact tone that he hoped
wouldn't show too much interest.

Cookie looked up from his scrubbing.
"Feller just disappeared one day. Left his gear
hangin' in the bunkhouse. Rode off and never
came back. Billy found his horse down at Bald
Mountain, but wasn't no sign of that cowboy."

Cookie walked out the back door to toss
out his dishwater, leaving Dan with a knot
in his stomach. The cook had all but admitted
that Jake killed the young cowboy. Now Dan's
dilemma had deepened. It wasn't his nature
to ignore the woman's plight. Championing
causes had gotten Dan into trouble plenty of
times. How could he turn his back on what
was happening to Jane?

He started out of the cookshack, chewing
a cold biscuit and thinking about the woman
. . . and the young cowboy who had cut those
flowers for her, a boy who was most likely
dead as a result. Heading over to the corrals
where the postholes were needed, Dan pondered what he would do with the information

he had now. A glance toward the house revealed a saddled horse tied to the porch rail. Was Jake in there now, slapping Jane for coming outside to help with the wounded man? Had she lied to Jake about it, the way Dan had? A lie that only made matters worse after Jake found her footprints?

Dan picked up the rock bar and went to work on the hole he hadn't finished yesterday. The iron bar rang loudly when it struck solid rock and Dan wondered if the racket would bring Jake outside, perhaps to confront Dan with the lie he told last night. Perhaps to make a try at handing Dan the same fate as the boy who cut the flowers last spring. Dan wondered if he should have worn his gun this morning. One thing was painfully clear to Dan now — working for Jake Logan wasn't going to be an ordinary job for day wages. Maybe he should pull out today before he got in any deeper into affairs that weren't his.

Minutes later, while Dan was pounding away at the bed of limestone, he glimpsed Jake coming out on the porch. Jake aimed a look toward the corrals where Dan labored, then swung up on his bay and rode off to the south, glancing over his shoulder once before he rode out of sight.

Dan wondered if Jake had hurt her. He remembered that the cook was close by, making it too dangerous to walk over to the cabin to inquire about Jane's circumstances. But the longer Dan worked on the posthole, the more he worried about what had happened to the woman. The voice of his conscience nagged at him. Hadn't he been the one to call Jane outside in the first place? To help with the injured man?

"Wouldn't be much I could do about it," he decided, slamming the bar into the hole with unneeded force while he thought about things. "Unless she's hurt real bad."

Between stabs with the rock bar, Dan glanced toward the front of the cabin, deliberating. If Jake caught him near the house, it might go even harder for Jane, and for Dan to boot. Finding out that Jake was the jealous type made the undertaking more risky.

I reckon if she wants my help, she'll ask for it, he told himself. She'll find a way to get word to me that she needs a helping hand to get clear of here. If she does, then I'll do anything I can to help her escape. If she don't ask, then it's none of my affair even if it does seem wrong, he thought. I could tell her that I'd be willing to help her get away if that's what she wanted. That way, the decision would be up to her. I wouldn't be meddling in her business.

He understood the danger of helping Jane

escape from the ranch. Logan would follow them, maybe with a couple of men such as Tom and Billy. There'd be a fight over it, likely a one-sided fight with the odds stacked against Dan. But that was one thing Dan Willis had always taken a certain amount of pride in — he never backed away from a fight or turned his back on someone who needed help. Lately his luck had been running bad and he didn't have much help to give a stranger beyond his willingness to give it. But helping Jane get away from Jake Logan's cruelty was something Dan could manage, even with empty pockets.

The longer he watched the silent cabin, the more worried he became about what might have happened to Jane. When he looked over to the cookshack he saw no one out and about in the midmorning heat. Could he risk slipping around to the back to tap on a window? And would Jane answer his knock if he did?

Compounding things, a herd of cattle that was probably stolen was headed for the ranch. More of Jake's men would be around the place then, making it even harder to find out what had happened to the woman with the place crawling with cowhands. Did he dare chance it? What would he find?

Sweat poured down Dan's face from his hatband. The bar had grown much heavier after the heavy slamming he'd done with it to help get rid of his anger. When he looked at the cabin, nothing moved behind any of the windows, and in his mind's eye he saw Jane lying on the floor with bloody bruises on her face. "Stop thinkin' about her, Willis," he scolded. "You'll get yourself worked up over it and there ain't a damn thing you can do."

Toward noon, he dropped the bar and walked to the cookshack to get some bacon grease for the blisters forming on his hands. As he neared the shack, he heard snoring coming from a back window of the kitchen. Walking quietly on the balls of his feet, he peered through the back door and found Cookie asleep on a wooden cot against one wall. Dan's mind went to work at once. He glanced toward the cabin. I could slip up to one of those windows now, he thought. Nobody'd see me.

He hurried away from the cookshack and trotted past the corrals to go around to the back of the house. When he neared the porch, the dog gave a low growl, forcing Dan to make a wider swing through a stand of live oaks to avoid the dog's jaws. At the back of the cabin he halted, for the dog made a circle too, snarling, warning Dan to keep his distance. Dan picked up a rock and tossed it against the rear door. The stone clattered on the back steps, and when there was no response, he threw another rock and called out, "Jane!"

The dog snarled more savagely at the sound of his voice, its hair bristling down its back. Then a sound from the back door silenced the dog. The door opened a crack, but it was too dark inside the cabin for Dan to see anything clearly.

Dan looked around him, then he spoke. "I just wanted to see if you were okay, ma'am," he said.

No one answered.

"Are you hurt?" he asked, peering into the darkness behind the door. "I've been worryin' that he might have hurt you, Miz Logan," Dan continued. "Everybody's gone, 'cept for Cookie, and he's sound asleep."

Slowly, the door opened a little wider. Then Dan saw Jane standing to one side of the door. "Go away from here, Dan!" she said in a soft voice that was strangely muffled. "You don't have a stake in any of this!"

Dan shook his head side to side. "You're right about not having a stake in things," he said, "but if you was to ask, I'd be willing to help you out of a fix. A man hadn't oughta hit a woman, Miz Logan, not for no reason on earth. If you take the notion that you want to go someplace else, I'll help you, ma'am. That's really about all I wanted to tell you. If you ain't bad hurt, then I'll be on my way back to them postholes."

"I'm . . . okay," she replied quietly, although Dan didn't like the sound of it.

"Remember what I said, Miz Logan," Dan added as he turned away from the back door. "I'm offerin' you my help to leave this place, if you take the notion. Jake don't scare me. When you get to know me a little better, you'll know that I can handle myself in a tight spot, and I'm a decent shot with a gun when I need to use one."

"I'm very grateful," Jane answered, still hidden in the shadows behind the door, "but you don't know Jake. He's . . . a killer, Dan. I appreciate what you've offered to do. You don't understand what Jake and his men are like. I can handle this alone."

There was something very different about the sound of her voice. "Are you sure you're all right?" he asked again, taking a step closer to the back door. "Your voice sounds kinda strange . . ."

"You'd better go," she said. "Before Jake comes back."

Dan halted and gave his surroundings a quick examination. "Ain't nobody around, ma'am," he said. "You'll have to forgive the fact that I'm bein' so nosy, but I had this suspicion that Jake hurt you last night. You see, he asked me if I'd talked to you, and I lied and said I hadn't. But Billy said Jake knew about how you came outside because he found your footprints around the spot where Bob was lyin'. So I reckon I'm already in trouble with Jake for not tellin' him the truth. But I done like you told me . . . I never admitted to sayin' a word to you. I lied, so he wouldn't put any more of them purple bruises on your cheek."

A silence between them lingered and it puzzled Dan. Then the door opened even wider and Jane stepped to the edge of the doorframe where the sunlight showed her face. "Are you satisfied?" she asked, when Dan's look became a stare. "This is what Jake does to me when I talk to another man, and that's why I'm leaving this place just as soon as I can."

Jane's lips were swollen, crusted over with dried blood. Her right eye was puffy, almost closed. The front of her blouse was torn and she held it closed with her hand.

"Good Lord," Dan said softly, barely above a whisper. He took a deep breath and tried to swallow, but his mouth felt like it was full of sand. "If you'll pardon me for sayin' so, Miz Logan, but you look awful." Then Dan's hands balled into fists. "Your husband needs to be hogtied, ma'am, to hit a woman like that. The way I was raised, Jake ain't no man at all. A man wouldn't do such a thing. He's a coward . . . there ain't no other word for it. You can't stay here, you've got to get away from Jake." Dan finally worked up enough spit so he could swallow. "And I'm just the feller to help you, Miz Logan. Like I told you before, I ain't scared of Jake. I can help you get to El Paso, since that's the way I was headed when I stopped off here. But you can't stay here and that's a natural fact. You said you aimed to leave soon as you could. Just want you to know I'll be ready whenever you say the word."

Jane came slowly down the back steps, looking both ways before she walked up to Dan and stared into his eyes. In bright sunlight, the injuries to her face looked even worse. "Jake will kill you if he finds us together," she said, her voice strained with emotion, a tear forming in each eye. "You'd be putting your life on the line for someone you hardly know, a woman who is another man's wife. I can't figure why you'd do it . . . for me."

For reasons he couldn't explain, Dan wanted to put his arms around her just then, but he held his arms at his sides. "I reckon it has to do with what's right and wrong," he answered. "My pa called it having principles. Fact is, you're in trouble. And I'll lend you a hand, mainly because you need help right now. That's the honest truth. Got no other reason to give you."

Jane's brow furrowed while she gave Dan an appraising look. "There are things you should know about me," she said. "This isn't the time or the place to tell you. Maybe one of these nights, after Jake goes to sleep, we'll talk about it. I've been making my own plans to leave Jake, after the cattle arrive at the end of the week. They drive them down to Mexico, and Jake goes with the herd." Now she searched Dan's face carefully. "I tried to leave Jake once before. He followed me and brought me back. But this time, I'll make sure he can't find me. This time I'm not coming back, no matter what . . ."

"I'll slip out of the bunkhouse at midnight," he said. "We can meet over yonder by the corrals. Nobody'll see us in those trees."

"I'll come if I can," she whispered.

Dan stood a little straighter and put some authority in his voice. "You can take one thing to the bank, Miz Logan. I'll help you get away from here, an' if anybody tries to stop us I'll make 'em think twice. Ridin' good horses, with a head start, I can promise you a safe trip to El Paso or most anyplace else you take a notion to go."

A slow smile crossed Jane's face, a bit lopsided where her lips were puffy. "I may be a woman," she said quietly, "but I can take care of myself. If you change your mind, I'll understand." Then her smile faded. "I'm leaving this place, and I'll go alone if I have to. Jake found me before because I was careless. But I won't make the same mistake again."

She turned and ran back inside the house. Dan stood in his tracks until the door closed, then turned away and walked toward the unfinished postholes with his mind made up to help a lady in distress no matter what the consequences. Down deep, he knew that a gun made all men equal if they knew how to use one.

Chapter 7

The sky had turned dusky by the time Jake, Tom, and Billy rode into the ranch. Dan noticed that their horses were lathered, and that they'd come from the south.

I suspect they've been down toward Mexico, he thought, cleaning small rocks from the bottom of a posthole. Probably to scout the trail they'll use to drive the cattle to the border.

All afternoon he'd been toiling with the holes while his mind was elsewhere. He'd formed one plan and then another for the moment when he and Jane rode away from the ranch. With Jake and the others escorting the herd to Mexico, Dan figured to have a three-day head start before Jake realized that his wife was gone. Three days, possibly four, would be enough to cover a lot of country, enough to hide their tracks by riding stretches of rocky ground when they could find it. All in all, Dan felt sure of the plan, but only if

Jake accompanied the herd south. Dan worried that Jake might have grown suspicious when he found out that Jane had been talking to Dan. If Dan's plan stood any chances of working, Jake's suspicions would have to be laid to rest. Dan meant to stay as far from the cabin as he could over the next few days, to put Jake's mind at ease. Jake might think that the beating he gave Jane would be enough to discourage her from running off while he was away with the herd.

There was a potential hitch in the plan that kept worrying Dan throughout the afternoon. If Jake left someone to keep an eye on Jane while he was gone, that man would have to be silenced somehow. If Cookie was the man left in charge of things, Dan was sure that he could handle him. A stick of firewood would put the cook to sleep until he could be trussed up in the kitchen. But if Jake appointed either Tom or Billy to handle the chore, the risks would increase. Both men carried guns and Dan harbored no doubts that they knew how to use them.

Jake came walking toward Dan, after his horse was put away in one of the corrals. "Here comes trouble," Dan whispered, preparing what he would say if Jake confronted him with the lie he'd told about talking to Jane yesterday.

Jake eyed the postholes as he walked up to Dan. He grunted and seemed satisfied. Jake's dark-whiskered face revealed nothing until he spoke.

"Time we had a talk, Mister Smith," he said. His voice was a deep growl.

Dan dropped the bar and shovel, adopting a look of surprise that he hoped would seem innocent. "Them holes are plenty deep, boss," he said.

Jake shook his head. His right hand rested on the butt of his Colt. "That ain't what we're gonna talk about," he said gruffly. "You lied to me last night, an' I won't tolerate a liar on my payroll. You said you didn't see a woman come out of the house when Bob showed up, an' that's a goddamn lie! Jane told me she gave you those blankets for the back of the wagon."

Dan began to wag his head side to side, but he knew Jake had him cold. Jake had beaten a confession out of his wife last night, after he found Jane's footprints. It would only worsen Jane's circumstances to deny what had happened. "She made me promise I wouldn't tell you that she came out," Dan replied softly, looking down at his boots. "Fact is, boss, she was scared to death to lend me a hand with that wounded gent. She handed me those blankets and then she ran back to the house like

81

her tailfeathers was on fire. Scaredest woman I ever met. I still can't figure out what she was so scared of, but she wouldn't stay to help me. She acted real strange about it. Said I couldn't tell you about the blankets." Dan swallowed. "I make it a habit to mind my own business. I was hired to dig postholes and that's all I aim to do around here, unless you've got a better job waitin' for me when I'm done with this corral. Truth is, I can sure use a job through the winter, Mister Logan, an' I'm the kind of feller who knows how to keep his mouth shut about things. You already warned me, and once is enough for me. If you'll ask around over in Sonora, you'll find out I never talked to anybody 'cept that dentist, and the undertaker. If I was the loose-lipped kind, I'd have gone to the sheriff about that dead feller I brought to town. But that sheriff'll tell you that Dan Smith never said a word about what happened out here."

Jake's expression changed a little, softening some. "You'd have made a big mistake if you had talked to the sheriff," he said, and a crooked smile widened his face. Then he looked Dan up and down, and his smile disappeared. "If you ever lie to me again, Dan, I'll blow a hole in your belly big enough to drive a wagon through. And if you ever talk to my wife again, there'll be the same result.

I never give a feller two chances. You lie to me again, or get near my wife, and you'll be buzzard food."

Jake glared at Dan, then turned on his heels and stalked off toward the cabin. Dan watched Jake's back until he climbed the porch steps, wondering if Jane was about to receive another beating from her husband.

Dan's backbone stiffened when he heard the cabin door close. "If I ever met a feller who deserves a killin', that's him," Dan whispered, flexing his hands unconsciously.

He started for the bunkhouse to wash up for supper, but his mind was still on Jake and what he had done to Jane the night before. It was hard to figure, what a woman like Jane was doing with a man like Jake. The more Dan thought about it, the less he could make of it. She seemed like a gentlewoman, so what was she doing married to a cruel bastard who used his fists on her?

Somethin' don't add up, Dan thought, trudging past the cookshack to the bunkhouse. Maybe that's what Jane aims to tell me about her . . . how she wound up with a no-good owlhoot like Jake.

Then Dan remembered the promise Jake had made him, to blow a hole in Dan's belly. "That may be a little harder to do than he figures," Dan said coldly, climbing the bunkhouse steps to get a change of clothing.

Tom was seated on his bunk when Dan walked in. Billy was nowhere around. Tom glared at Dan, and Dan knew the fistfight between them was not forgotten.

"Evenin', Tom," Dan said, heading for his war bag, hoping that polite conversation might take Tom's mind off his sore jaw. The last thing Dan needed right now was more trouble at the ranch. Jake was looking for an excuse to send Dan on his way and another scrap with Tom would give him reason enough.

"Wasn't expectin' that first punch you landed," Tom said. "It was a lucky punch, afore I was ready. In a fair fight, I can whip your ass, cowboy."

Dan continued past Tom to his bunk. "I say we let it rest, Tom. Forget about it. Maybe it was a lucky punch after all. I won't be the one to argue it."

"You whupped me in front of Billy," Tom growled, standing up behind Dan's back, "an' it wasn't no fair fight. I aim to square things between us — I'll show you who's got the best swing, you scarecrow son of a bitch!"

Dan turned around and raised both palms. "Not here, Tom," he protested. "The bossman ain't in the best mood just now. We can settle it when he ain't around."

Tom's shoulders were bunched and his fists

84

were doubled. Dan could plainly see the fire in his eyes. "Are you backin' down?" Tom asked, jutting his chin.

Backing down from Tom would have stuck in Dan's craw under most circumstances, but with bigger things at stake, he decided to let the cowboy have his way. "I reckon you could say that," Dan said, even though the words had a bitter taste. "I need this job. I'm flat broke. I'd rather back down than get fired off this ranch."

Tom still glowered at Dan. "You gotta say it so Billy can hear it," he said. "Just my word against yours otherwise."

Dan could feel his cheeks turning hot. Tom was pushing it, to have things made public. If it hadn't been for the woman, Dan would never have allowed Tom's challenge to go unmet, public or private. "Okay, Tom. I'll tell Billy you backed me down."

Tom's fists relaxed, then he let his arms hang at his sides. "I can whup you fair an' square," he said. "You hit me when I wasn't expectin' it . . . caught me off my guard."

"Have it any way you want it," Dan replied. "I need to make a payday."

A leer broadened Tom's face. "Jake knows you had words with his wife," he said softly, enjoying himself. "Said this afternoon that he was gonna use a gun on you if it happened again. Said he aimed to warn you about it, and he'd put you six feet under if you got near her again. So you'd best mind your manners around here, cowboy, or you'll be fillin' a shallow grave. Jake's real handy with a six-shooter. One of the best."

"I'm not lookin' for any trouble," Dan said, reaching for his war bag on a peg above his bunk. "All I did was ask the lady to help me with that gent who had the bullet hole. She handed me a pile of blankets and went back inside. Hardly said a word to me."

Tom let out a dry chuckle. "Jake said he'd break her of that habit," he remarked, as though he agreed with what Jake had done to her. "A woman's like a cold-jawed bronc anyway. You gotta teach 'em to obey."

Tom made a turn for the door and sauntered out. Dan waited until Tom was away from the bunkhouse before he carried a clean shirt out to the windmill for his evening bath. Peeling off his grime-caked clothing when he was alone beside the pump jack, Dan felt his anger cool. Backing down from Tom had taken every ounce of control he had been able to muster. "I had to do it," he told himself as he began to work the pump handle. "Jake woulda sent me packin' if I'd gotten myself in a scrape with Tom."

While he washed himself, he thought about

the risks of meeting Jane tonight at midnight near the corrals. He knew he would have to slip out of the bunkhouse very quietly, when the Big Dipper pointed to midnight, and make doubly sure that his footsteps did not alert the spotted dog. If Jake, or one of the men, caught Dan and Jane together in the dark, there would be hell to pay and the shooting would start before Dan was ready. And there was another problem to consider, one that needed a remedy before Dan helped Jane make her escape. Dan had just four bullets for his Colt, and no shells for his rifle. He desperately needed cartridges for both guns so he'd have a chance to fight off the pursuit that would result when Jake discovered what had happened. Jake would come after them hard and fast, most likely with a handful of men. It would come down to a horse race of sorts, but with even a couple of days for a head start, Dan was sure they could reach El Paso before Jake caught up to them.

"When we get there, I'll tell the Texas Rangers what's goin' on out here," he said softly, soaping his arms and face. "Jake'll have his hands full with the law and he'll be too busy to bother Jane when I tell an honest lawman about the cattle rustling."

They would have better than two hundred miles of rough, dry country to cross before they reached El Paso. Only a few tiny settlements lay in between, spots on the map named Fort Stockton and Balmorhea near the rugged Davis Mountains. Information about the road to El Paso had been hard to come by, sketchy at best. Everyone he talked to had agreed that it was a dangerous journey, across the lands of the Comanche and Apache where it was rumored that renegade bands still rode the empty mountains, preying on unsuspecting travelers between the scattered army posts.

"We could tell the army what Jake has been up to," he said later, rinsing off the soap, thinking out loud. "We'd be safe at an army post until the Rangers got there. That way, we wouldn't have nearly so many miles to cover before the woman was safe."

He decided, as he dried himself off, that he'd tell Jane about his plans tonight, hoping she would feel better about things when she heard his ideas for making the escape. Then he wondered if Jane would look with favor on his notion to tell the Texas Rangers about the rustling operation. She was still Jake's wife, making Dan wonder how she would feel about putting her husband in jail.

"Maybe she won't like that part," he said, pulling on his worn boots. "Could be all she wants is to get away from him. Hard to figure how a woman will think when it comes to something like that. I reckon she can decide when the time comes."

A lantern burned in the cookshack window as Dan started away from the windmill. Smoke curled away from the stovepipe, and for the time being Dan forgot about everything else, putting his mind on supper. Walking past the horse pens, he glanced over the top rail at his buckskin.

"You're fillin' up already, Buck," he said, grinning when he saw how the animal's flanks had rounded. "Better eat everything you can get your muzzle around, old hoss, 'cause we've got a hell of a long road ahead of us in a few days, and we're gonna have to make the trip in a hurry."

Then Dan passed his glance over the rest of the geldings in the pen, hoping to find one long-muscled horse in the bunch that would have some speed and stamina. Jane's horse would have to be as good as Buck when it came to endurance and toughness, and a bit of early speed wouldn't hurt matters either.

He spied a chestnut with its head lowered near the back fence of the pen. The horse had a deep heartgirth and a long barrel that would give it long strides. Muscles bulged in the chestnut's gaskins, a sign of power in a good horse, and the gelding's croup was lengthy enough to balance it with the rest of the animal's conformation. "That chestnut is the one we'll take," Dan said softly. "Him an' Buck are just what we need to put some distance between us and this cattle spread. If I'm any judge of horseflesh, they won't catch us aboard those two geldings yonder. Not if we've got a decent lead."

His nose was greeted by wonderful smells when he walked into the cookshack. Right off, his belly began to rumble. He saw Tom look up when he approached the table.

"Tell Billy what you said," Tom demanded gruffly.

Swallowing his pride, Dan said, "I backed down from another fight with your pardner, Billy. I'm in enough trouble with the boss the way it is. Tom claims it was a lucky punch I throwed when I took him off his feet."

Dan felt Billy's stare as he took a tin plate and filled it with stew. When Dan met Billy's gaze, he knew something was wrong with the way the cowboy was looking at him, like he didn't believe a word of what Dan said about backing down from Tom.

All through the meal, Billy made it plain that he was suspicious of Dan's refusal to fight Tom. Billy kept looking at Dan, and one time he just shook his head like he knew something didn't add up.

Chapter 8

The moon hung like a silver disk above the live oak grove. All around the trees the ranch was quiet. Dan waited in the shadows with his heart pounding. It had taken all the stealth he could manage to slip out of the bunkhouse unnoticed, but now, as he waited for Jane in the dark, he began to worry about Jake Logan. If Jake suspected Jane was up to something, he might follow her outside after pretending to be asleep. Just in case there was trouble, Dan wore his gunbelt. Out in the moonlight, he had checked the loads carefully, making sure a cartridge was to the left of the hammer for the moment when he fired. With time on his hands, waiting for Jane to slip out of the cabin, Dan worried that four shells might not be enough. If Billy and Tom ran out to get in the fracas, Dan would have to make doubly sure of each shot. . . . His life, and Jane's, might depend on good aim taken hastily in the darkness.

An owl hooted somewhere in the trees and the sound made Dan flinch. "Damn, I'm jumpy," he whispered, scanning the dark around him, listening for the slightest noise that might signal the beginning of trouble. Staring up through the tree limbs, he guessed the time to be midnight by the position of the Big Dipper, the way a trail hand tells time when he rides night herder. He touched his chest with his fingertips, feeling his own heartbeat, then grinned. "Take it easy, Willis," he told himself, as he examined the shadows around the cabin. "Nothin' to worry about."

A coyote howled in the distance, barking four times, then sending its eerie cry into the night sky. The sound made Dan shiver. In the dry grass near his feet, a cricket chirped, distracting him briefly.

Behind the cookshack, a horse snorted softly in one of the corrals. Dan noticed a tiny tremor in his fingertips and he laughed inwardly at himself. "It's this waitin'," he said quietly, watching the shadows again, his gaze lingering when he saw a shape he didn't recognize.

He was far enough from the cabin to keep the dog from hearing his approach, and he decided things were set about as well as they could be, under the circumstances. Jane had said she would come if she could. He decided he would wait, perhaps an extra hour if need be, before he gave up and went back to bed.

Suddenly he saw a shadow move behind the house. A figure crept quietly across the moonlit grass, and behind the shadow Dan saw the dog moving slowly. Dan's hand fell to the butt of his Colt. His palm was wet with sweat, clammy around the walnut grips as he watched the figure slip soundlessly into the trees. As a precaution, he hid behind an oak trunk and waited. Listening to the soft footfalls approach, he held his breath until the sounds were very close.

"Dan?" A soft feminine whisper called.

"Over here," he replied quietly, then stepped around the tree to show himself.

Jane hurried over, halting close to his chest. "I had to be sure Jake was sound asleep," she said. "He was in a foul mood before he went to bed, worrying about what Bob Huffman said."

He could smell the fragrance of her hair, and in patches of moonlight slanting between the tree limbs, he caught glimpses of her face.

"What does it mean . . . that there was a double-cross?" he asked.

"That's what is worrying Jake. He's wondering if Amos Cade went to the law someplace, after Jake cut him out of a deal. Amos was boiling mad when Jake ran him off last month. Jake swore he'd kill Amos if he didn't clear out and keep his mouth shut."

Dan cleared his throat. "I figure it's about time you told me exactly what's goin' on around here," he said.

Jane nodded. "Jake's men are thinning herds up north, taking just a few at a time from different ranches. They drive the cattle down here and change the brands, then Jake makes arrangements to sell them across the border in Mexico. Down there, nobody asks any questions when the price is right. Jake has been running the operation for a couple of years now. The Sutton County sheriff takes a payoff to look the other way, and he keeps anybody from getting too close to the ranch. He makes a show of investigating complaints, to keep himself in the clear if anyone shows up trailing the stolen cattle."

Dan shook his head. "That's about the way I had it figured," he said. "Only thinning the herds is smarter than rustling too big a bunch." Then Dan frowned. "So what's a pretty lady like you doin' here in the middle of a rustling operation?"

"It's a long story. Are you sure you want to hear it?"

"Yes, ma'am, I surely do," he answered. "It's been a puzzlement why you're involved with a man like Jake Logan."

Jane took a deep breath. She turned slightly,

so she wasn't looking at Dan any longer. "I met Jake five years ago," she began in a far-away voice. "He was big and handsome, and a real gentleman, or so I thought. He told me he was in the ranching business, and he asked me to marry him one time when he came to Fort Worth. I saw it as my chance to escape the kind of life I'd been leading." She gave Dan a sideways look. "You see, Dan, I was running a string of girls. I was a madam, and before that, I . . ." Her voice trailed off as she watched Dan's face for his reaction.

"You mean . . . you was runnin' a whore-house?" he asked. The idea left him dumb-struck. Jane didn't look like the type at all, not like the crib matrons he'd seen inside Waco's whorehouses.

She waited a moment before she answered him. "Yes, Dan. I ran a whorehouse in Hell's Half Acre. It was called the Crystal Palace. I went to work there when I was sixteen."

Dan had trouble arranging his thoughts. It didn't seem possible that Jane had been in-volved in that sort of thing. "Why would a nice lady like you work in a place like that?" he asked.

"I didn't choose it, if that's what you mean," she said softly, with a hint of sadness. "My folks were very poor. Our wagon broke down outside of Fort Worth while we were on our way to California. My pa took a job where he could find work. They hired him to mop the floors and clean out spittoons at the Crystal Palace. Pa got killed a few weeks later when a gunfight broke out inside the saloon. My ma couldn't find work and we were about to starve. Rose Parker owned the Crystal Palace, and she told me how I could make a lot of money, working upstairs. I didn't want to do it, but I didn't think I had a choice. We had to survive, me and my ma. I had to do something." Jane looked up at the stars and sighed. "Later, I thought marrying Jake Logan was a way out for me. I didn't know what he was like, and right then, I didn't care. So here I am now, a prisoner locked up inside that little cabin, just to please Jake whenever he wants me. But I've been making plans to get myself out of this mess, and one way or another, I will."

Hearing Jane's sad story had softened Dan's reaction some. When he first heard her frank admission that she worked in a whorehouse, he'd been too shocked to see another side of it. "I said I'd help you, and I will," he began. "It don't matter about your past. I growed up real poor myself, but I reckon a man's got more choices when it comes to a profession."

Jane squared her shoulders and turned to face him. "Don't judge me," she said, and there was an edge to her voice. "I know who I am, and who I was. I made a choice back then, and I've learned to live with it. I made another bad choice when I married Jake, but I won't spend the rest of my life paying for it. When Jake leaves with that herd, I'm pulling out. Alone, if I have to, but my mind's made up." She lifted her chin, and her eyes narrowed. "And before I'm finished with Jake, he'll regret the things he's done to me. I'm going to put a stop to his crooked dealings and have him put away behind bars, where he belongs!"

Dan stood silently for a moment, reading the woman's face. "I reckon you just answered a question I had," he said. "I'd aimed to find an honest lawman between here and El Paso so I could tell him about what I suspicioned was going on here. I wondered how you'd feel about it, seein' as Jake is your husband. Jake and his bunch oughta be stopped, rustling from hardworking ranchers the way they are. There's an army post on the way to El Paso, and you'd be safe from Jake there. We could tell the post commander about the rustling. That would put the soldiers on his trail and most likely a wire to the Texas Rangers, to boot."

Jane's gaze was unwavering when she answered Dan. "Jake has to be stopped. He's a killer, and a cattle thief," she said quickly. "But it will be dangerous, leaving here," she whispered. "Jake will come after me when he finds out I've gone. He followed me once before, and when he discovers that you helped me get away, he'll try to kill you. He's a dangerous man. He won't let anything stop him until he finds me, unless the law can stop him first."

Dan rocked back gently on his boot heels. "A bullet will stop most anybody, Miz Logan," he said. "If Jake forces my hand, I'll have no choice but to use my gun."

Jane reached out and touched his arm. "I still don't know why you are willing to risk your life for me. You said it had something to do with having principles, but having principles isn't enough to explain why you'd help someone like me, a woman you hardly know."

"It's what my pa would have done," Dan replied. "He taught me what's right and what's wrong. A man who uses his fists on a woman needs to be reminded of his manners, an' that a woman don't wear a brand either. You've got a right to decide for yourself if you stay someplace. Your husband ain't nothin' but a coward, Miz Logan, to hit you the way he does."

"Please call me Jane," she said softly, smiling again. "I barely know you, Dan Smith, but I already know that you're a brave man and a gentleman."

Dan chuckled. "My name's Dan Willis. You guessed right the first time we met — my name ain't Smith. And I'll help you get away from this ranch, Jane. I've been planning the best time to ride out of here, and it seems real simple. When Jake and the others head south with that herd of cattle, we'll saddle a good horse for you and clear out as fast as we can."

Jane's face darkened with worry. "Jake leaves Billy here to keep an eye on me when he rides to the border. Billy watches me real close. Jake trusts him, and Billy is good with a gun. Jake told me that Billy was a gunfighter, a paid gun up in Kansas Territory a few years back, until the law put out warrants for his arrest. We'll have to think of a way to get past Billy. I'd been planning to leave during the night, while Billy was asleep. It would be morning before he noticed that I took a horse. By then, I'd be far enough from here that he couldn't catch me."

It was bad news, that Billy was the one left behind to guard Jane. Billy was the most cautious of the pair of cowboys at the ranch, and he wore a gunfighter's rig. "Maybe I can knock Billy out cold and tie him up," Dan suggested. "Catch him while he's sleepin' and bang him over the head. Tie his feet and hands." He thought of another problem. "What about the cook? Does he stay behind, or go with the herd?"

"Jake takes him along to feed the hands," she replied. "Billy's the only one who stays."

"I need to get my hands on some forty-four caliber ammunition before we ride out," Dan said. "I've been down on my luck lately," he added, feeling some embarrassment. "Got just four bullets for my Colt an' no shells for my rifle. Four slugs won't be enough."

Jane frowned. "Jake keeps boxes of cartridges in the house. I can take a box from the gun cabinet and he'll never know the difference. And don't worry, Dan. I've got some money stashed away where Jake can't find it. I saved a little here and there, for the time when I knew I'd be on my own."

"Can you ride a horse?" he asked. "I mean really ride a horse, just in case we find ourselves in a horse race?"

She shook her head, and gave him a look of mock indignation. "I can ride as well as any man. If you put me to the test, I'll prove it to you."

He grinned when he heard the determination in her voice. "I had you figured for a tough lady," he said. Then the smile left his face. "You'd have to be tough . . . to take what you've taken from Jake."

"I've been biding my time," she said softly. Then she stared up at the sky. "Right at first, I hoped things would work out. I didn't want to go back to the Crystal Palace . . . back to that kind of life. But Jake, he only got meaner. I discovered that I didn't really know him at all. Then I found out about the cattle rustling. He had lied to me all along. He never was a rancher. I found an old poster at the bottom of his trunk, the one he keeps at the foot of the bed. He left it unlocked, and I went through it. The poster offered a five-hundred-dollar reward for the arrest of Jake Logan, and the charge was murder, Dan! He killed a man down in Galveston, according to the circular. That's how I found out my husband is a killer, and I've got proof he's a cattle thief. I've been a witness to the changing of those brands ever since he brought me down here."

"You can tell the Rangers what you saw," Dan said. "It'll be enough to put Jake behind bars, where he can't bother you again."

Jane turned her face to Dan's, and when a shaft of moonlight struck her features, the swelling around her eye and the scabs on her lips, he reached for her and held her shoulders. "You're a tough little lady," he said gently. "Just a few more days, and you won't have to worry about Jake. You've got my word on it."

Suddenly, the dog whimpered. It was looking toward the cabin. Dan was puzzled by the dog's behavior, until he saw something move near one corner of the house. "Someone's out there," he whispered.

Jane stiffened in his grasp, then she whirled around and froze.

"It's Jake," she gasped, clapping her hands over her mouth to silence her voice. She looked over her shoulder at Dan. "Get back to the bunkhouse," she whispered, her arms trembling. "I'll tell Jake I came outside for a walk in the moonlight. Hurry! Before he finds you here!"

Dan wheeled around, then hesitated. "If he don't believe you, then he might —"

She was shaking her head back and forth before he could finish. He wanted to stay and help her . . . even kill Jake, if he threatened to hurt her again.

"No!" she whispered. "I can take care of myself. We can't let him find us together. Not now! It might ruin everything."

Without choices, Dan started for the bunkhouse on the balls of his feet, keeping to the shadows beneath the trees to hide his progress away from the corrals. His heart was beating like a drum when he hurried past the back of the cookshack, but his right hand was curled around his pistol grips.

He crept quietly into the bunkhouse. Billy and Tom were both snoring. He lowered himself onto his bunk and pulled a thin blanket over himself, then, as an afterthought, drew his Colt .44/.40 and rested it across his stomach beneath the bed cover.

Chapter 9

First there were footsteps across the hardpan in front of the bunkhouse. Soft, gentle footfalls, made by a man who did not want to be heard. Above the snores of the two cowboys in the bunks near the door, Dan heard someone enter the room. Then the sounds stopped, and for a time, there were only the snores.

Dan held his breath and waited. His palm grew sweaty around his gun butt. He opened his eyelids just a crack and tried to see through the darkness. Moonlight poured through a bunkhouse window, forming a silver square on the bunkhouse floor. But the rest of the room was too dark and he couldn't see anything.

Time flowed slow as molasses from a jug on a winter day. Still holding his breath, Dan waited, listening for the slightest sound, piercing the darkness near the doorway for the smallest movement. He knew it was Jake who had entered the bunkhouse. But why was Jake standing there? What was he waiting for? Was he listening to the snores? Counting them?

Dan gave what might pass for a snore, more a ragged intake of breath through his nose that rattled slightly. Remaining motionless, he peered through cracked eyelids and waited.

Then a boot scraped across the room. Dan saw a shadowy outline moving toward him. Dan's hand tightened around his Colt, though he knew he dared not lift the barrel toward his target . . . not yet, for the movement beneath the bed cover would be a dead giveaway that Dan was not asleep.

The figure entered the patch of moonlight from the window and Dan saw Jake clearly. A gun gleamed in Jake's fist as the moonlight struck its metal surface. Jake came slowly, quietly, toward Dan's bunk with his gun drawn.

This is it, Willis, Dan thought. You're gonna die right here in bed unless you do something first. He aims to kill you, most likely because he just beat the truth out of his wife again.

Jake halted at the foot of Dan's bunk. Even through his eyelashes, Dan could see the darker muzzle of Jake's pistol. Dan's mind was racing. Did he dare risk waiting until he heard the click of a cocking six-shooter before he brought his own weapon up for a shot? Time seemed frozen. Dan was sure his life hung in the balance and his next move, or the lack of one, would decide whether he lived or died. He also reasoned that his first shot at Jake would bring Billy and Tom flying off their bunks, clawing for their guns to enter the fight. Dan had just four chances to kill three gunmen once the shooting started, and only a few precious seconds to get the job done.

Jake stood at Dan's feet, rock-still, as if he couldn't decide what to do for the moment. Dan figured to risk another deep breath, the kind a sleeping man sometimes takes, hoping it would fool Jake into thinking Dan was a light sleeper.

He heard Jake grunt, and the sound almost made Dan flinch, until Dan caught himself.

"If I didn't need them goddamn holes so bad," Jake muttered. "If the boys weren't bringin' so many cows this time . . ."

Dan saw Jake lower his pistol. It seemed an eternity before Jake turned away from Dan's bed and started back across the room, making no effort now to walk quietly. The sounds of Jake's boots disturbed Billy. Billy jerked upright on his bunk and tossed his covers aside, reaching for his gunbelt hanging from a corner of the bed frame.

"It's me, Billy," Jake growled hoarsely. "Go back to sleep. I was just checkin' on things down here. Thought I saw somebody sneak through this door a while ago. Figured it was the new hand, pokin' around in things where he don't belong."

From the corner of his slitted eyes, Dan glimpsed Billy as the little gunman rubbed his face.

"You figger he's suspicious about our operation, boss?" Billy asked sleepily, glancing toward Dan's bunk.

"Can't say for sure," Jake grunted. "But Jane was outside, claimin' she only went for a walk in the moonlight, but she lied to me once 'bout talkin' to this newcomer."

Dan lay stock-still, listening, clasping his gun so tightly that his fingers hurt.

"Don't worry about Dan," Billy said softly. "He was layin' right where he is now when I drifted off. The skinny bastard is probably too tired from diggin' to care about much of anything, boss. If you want my opinion, I don't figure Dan's looking for trouble. Afore we went to bed, he backed down from a fight with Tom, on account of he told Tom that he needed this job real bad. Hell, boss, he'd be a fool to tangle with you. Even dumb as he is, I figure he's too smart for that."

Jake seemed satisfied and moved closer to the bunkhouse door. "I don't trust that damn woman no more," he growled, "but maybe

107

I was wrong about her and Dan. I reckon it wasn't nothin' this time. I hope not, because I can't afford to have too many bodies turning up down at Bald Mountain." Jake laughed softly, and the sound made Dan shiver.

"Nobody'll find that other kid," Billy said, lowering his voice. "I took care of it."

Tom's snoring halted abruptly. The cowboy stirred beneath his covers, then his snores resumed.

It was Jake who spoke next. "I've been worried about Amos," he said. "After what Bob told Dan about a double-cross. If Amos spilled his story to the Texas Rangers, we could be in a heap of trouble."

"Cade's too smart for that, boss," Billy remarked quietly. "He'd be up to his own neck in troubles. Hell, he rode with us for better'n a year. I'm guessing Bob meant that Cade went in business for himself, cutting herds by his lonesome, maybe even working some of the ranches we've been hitting. I warned you — you shoulda killed Cade. Or let me kill him. It was a mistake to let him just ride off."

Jake was silent a moment. "I figured he'd clear out of this country. I told him what would happen if I ever set eyes on him again."

"Appears he didn't pay much attention to what you said," Billy observed. "It's my guess that Cade was cutting a herd someplace when

Bob rode up on him. Cade shot him, but Bob got clear before Cade could make sure he finished the job."

"Just so Amos didn't go to the law," Jake whispered. "We'll be in a jam if a bunch of lawmen show up while we've got those mixed-brand cattle in the pens." Jake sighed. "You go on and get some sleep, Billy. Keep an eye on that Dan Smith . . . watch him real close. Soon as that fence gets built, I'll hand him his wages and run him off. Until that fence goes up, watch Dan every chance you get. I don't trust nobody these days. This fall, we'll move our operation farther west, soon as the lease is up on this place. That's a lesson I learned a long time ago, Billy. Keep movin' around when you're in this business. Makes it harder for the law to pick up your trail."

Jake clumped out of the bunkhouse. Dan remained frozen, taking regular breaths so Billy could hear them. Minutes later, Billy was in bed and snoring again. Only then was Dan able to relax.

That was close, he thought, staring up at the dark ceiling. Now Dan knew for certain that Billy and Jake were involved in the murder of the young cowboy the previous spring. Dan had not only stumbled into the middle of a rustler's den, but the men were also cold-blooded murderers. Getting Jane away from

Jake would be no small undertaking. Even if they made it, Jake would be on their trail as soon as he learned what had happened. One thing was crystal clear now — Dan knew he would need plenty of cartridges for his pistol and his rifle. Down deep, Dan knew there would be a shoot-out before it was over, and a man with just four bullets didn't stand much of a chance of getting out of the fight with his skin.

He wondered whether he was playing the part of a fool. Jane was another man's wife. Staring blankly at the roof beams while Tom and Billy snored, he pondered the wisdom of getting involved in her flight. Was he sticking his neck in a noose because of his principles? Was that the real reason? Or was he secretly hoping that Jane might develop some feelings for him if he went to her aid?

He holstered his Colt, feeling confused about what was going on. Just before he dropped off to sleep, he wondered if he'd gone loco on the ride away from Waco. Did jackrabbit meat cause a man to have crazy notions if he ate too much of it?

Billy was watching him while he ate his breakfast, and the gunman's stare made Dan uncomfortable. Dan tried to put Billy's mind to rest with idle conversation.

"When that fence gets built, I'm headed straight to New Mexico Territory," he said, spooning eggs into his cheeks as he talked. "I hear they pay wages nigh onto thirty dollars a month out there for a man who can swing a loop an' catch what he's after with it. You ever been out there, Billy?"

Billy shook his head. Tom ignored the question, stuffing his mouth with food. Dan hoped the talk about New Mexico Territory would quiet Billy's suspicions, and maybe word would get back to Jake about Dan's plans.

"I was told it's right pretty country," Dan went on. "Big mountains. Lots of tall pine trees and plenty of grass. Sounds like a good place for a man to settle down, don't you think?"

Billy shrugged. "Depends on what a man wants for scenery, I reckon," he answered. "That thirty a month sounds good. Better'n wages in these parts, for a fact."

Dan shook his head. "I'll be leaving the very same day I get paid. With some money in my pockets, I can get out west in time to hire on for a fall roundup some place. In fact, I'll be in somethin' of a hurry. It's gettin' late in the year and I've got lots of miles to cover."

Tom gave Dan a disinterested look. "Won't nobody around here be sorry to see you pull out," he said, around a mouthful of eggs and bacon. "Me, I'll be damn glad to see you go, cowboy. You ain't been nothin' but a nuisance."

Dan forced a grin. "That ain't a very friendly attitude, Tom," he said, then went back to eating, letting the subject drop before he got mad over Tom's remark, though he could feel his ears turning red.

"Which way'd you aim to ride?" Billy asked, surprising Dan with the question.

"Fort Stockton, then Balmorhea," Dan blurted out, before he had time to think. Then a sinking feeling took away Dan's appetite. He had just informed Billy about the direction he and Jane would ride when they left the ranch. Hoping it wasn't already too late, Dan added, "But I was considerin' riding cross-country, maybe northwest so I could see them Guadalupe Mountains. Folks claim those big mountains are mighty pretty. Empty as all get-out too."

Billy did not look up from his plate, making Dan all the more sorry for revealing the road he meant to follow. Billy hadn't paid any attention to the Guadalupe Mountain story.

Dan let out a soft sigh and got up from the table. He plodded out the cookshack door as though a heavy weight rested on his shoulders. When Billy found Dan and Jane missing at the ranch, he would direct Jake down the road to Fort Stockton on account of Dan's careless remark.

"Damn," Dan whispered, trudging over to the unfinished postholes. He picked up the rock bar. "Maybe one of these days I'll learn to keep my mouth shut, if this wagging tongue don't get me killed beforehand."

Chapter 10

The day wore on with grueling sameness. Dan dug postholes in the unrelenting limestone until he felt sure he would collapse from exhaustion. Lifting the rock bar became a task almost beyond his capabilities by late afternoon, and when he shoveled loose stones from the bottom of a hole his arms shook so hard that he had trouble tossing the stones aside. Sweat plastered his shirt to his skin and poured into his eyes, requiring that he sleeve it away more frequently as the day passed. His belly rumbled with hunger. He took frequent drinks from the windmill, trembling so badly that he had a time holding the tin cup. Every muscle in his body ached with fatigue. He made an effort not to count the remaining holes to be dug, fearing that the knowledge might add to his misery.

A couple of hours before dark, while Dan rested on the handle of the shovel, he saw a rider galloping toward the ranch from the north. A cloud of dust was the first warning of the rider's approach and when Dan saw the caliche cloud, he squinted at it, frowning.

"Another feller in one hell of a hurry," he said under his breath. "Hope he ain't got a bullet hole in him too."

A lathered brown horse raced off a hilltop. Its rider was bent low over the horse's neck, whipping the reins across the animal's rump.

The brown galloped to the front of the cabin, where it was jerked to a sliding halt. Dust boiled around the horse and rider as the man aboard the brown dismounted. Spurs rattling, the cowboy ran to the porch steps as fast as he could travel.

"Jake! Jake!" the cowboy cried, boots thumping over the porch boards to the front door.

The door opened moments later. Dan recognized Jake's outline in the doorway.

"There's been some trouble," Dan heard the cowboy say.

Jake glanced toward the corrals, then admitted the cowboy into the cabin.

"Wonder what that was all about?" Dan said, scooping small rocks from the hole he was digging. The lathered brown gelding swung away from the house and trotted over to a water trough below the windmill to slake its thirst. Air whistled through its muzzle while it drank its fill.

Later, both men came back out on the porch. Jake pointed to the cookshack. The cowboy nodded and went down the steps to gather the reins on his horse, walking much slower now, as though something had been done about the reason for his haste.

Jake looked at Dan. For a time, they stared at each other as the newcomer led his horse toward the corrals. When the stare lasted too long, Dan went back to his digging, although he continued to look up now and then until Jake went back in the house. The newcomer tied his horse to the corral fence and began unsaddling at a leisurely pace. Apparently, whatever it was that had brought him to the ranch in an all-out run had been resolved.

Dan labored another hour, finishing one more hole. Then he put the tools aside and started toward the bunkhouse. Cookie's supper fire sent smoke into the evening sky, reminding Dan that he was hungry.

He walked in the bunkhouse and came face to face with the cowboy who had ridden in earlier. The man was slouched atop a vacant bunk, rolling a smoke. He looked up when Dan walked in. Dan noticed the gunbelt around the stranger's waist.

"Howdy," Dan said, pausing near the newcomer's bunk. "I'm Dan Smith. Just hired on the first of the week." He stuck out his hand.

The cowboy ignored the offer of a handshake. "Jake told me you found Bob Huffman," he said evenly, tipping tobacco into a piece of corn shuck from the mouth of a small cloth bag. "Jake said Bob told you it was Amos who shot him."

The cowboy's unfriendly tone made Dan cautious. "He didn't say Cade shot him," Dan explained. "He said to tell Jake that a gent by the name of Cade double-crossed him. He fell unconscious after that. I tried to get him to a doctor. He was dead by the time I got to Sonora."

The stranger's expression was flat and hard. His square-jawed face sported a week's growth of stubble. "Bob an' me was pardners," he said. "I aim to square things with Amos when I see him again." He licked the edges of the corn shuck and rolled his smoke, twisting the ends. "When Bob didn't show up at the meeting place with cattle, I knowed somethin' was wrong."

Dan shrugged and started for his bunk. The newcomer hadn't bothered to tell Dan his name, and he'd refused to shake hands when Dan introduced himself. It seemed that every cowboy in Jake's employ had a surly disposition.

He took down his war bag, only to discover that he had no more clean shirts. Removing his soiled clothing, he decided it was time to do a little washing at the water trough. But as he walked past the newcomer's bunk, the cowboy halted Dan with an uplifted hand.

"The name's Clay Weeks," he said, then struck a match on the frame of his bunk and held the flame to his smoke, still watching Dan with hooded eyes.

"Pleased to meet you, Clay," Dan replied. "Sorry 'bout what happened to your pardner. I did all I could to save him, but he'd lost too much blood."

"I'm obliged for what you tried to do for Bob," he said. "Bob was my friend. Amos don't know it yet, but he's as good as dead when I cross his trail."

Dan nodded. Clay seemed friendly enough now, and Dan decided to risk asking about the cattle herd. "When will the cattle get here?" he asked. "Just wonderin' how long I've got to finish that corral fence."

"Two days," Clay answered, blowing smoke toward the ceiling. "We waited for Bob at that canyon as long as we could. Ran out of grass day before yesterday. Got a big bunch this time . . . better'n two hundred head."

Dan was shocked by the size of the stolen herd. Two hundred cows would fetch a handsome price down in Mexico, even at rock-bottom figures. "That don't give me much time," Dan answered. "That's solid bedrock out yonder. The diggin's mighty slow."

Clay was watching him the way a cat watches a mouse. "You on the run from the law someplace?" he asked.

Dan shook his head. "On my way to New Mexico Territory to hire on with a cow outfit. My poke ran dry, so I stopped off here askin' for day wages."

Now Clay's eyes were filled with suspicion. "Then maybe I told you more'n I should," he said quietly. "I figured you was gonna ride with us from here on. That ain't like Jake . . . to hire an outsider."

Dan hooked his thumbs in his front pockets, wary of Clay's sudden change. "I'll be leavin' soon as that fence is done. No call to get a burr under your saddle. I mind my own business."

It was evident that Clay didn't like Dan's answer. He shook his head from side to side. "You could wind up dead if you don't," he said.

Dan let the subject drop and started for the door, but he could feel Clay's eyes on his back as he went outside. Swinging toward the windmill, he felt the hairs prickle down the back of his neck. If Dan was any judge of hard

119

men, Clay Weeks would make a deadly adversary. With men like Clay and Billy and Jake close on their heels when he and Jane left the ranch, there would be no room for mistakes. A gun battle with men of their ilk would be the toughest test Dan had ever faced. His aim would have to be near perfect if they got within range. A moment of carelessness would cost him his life.

"I must be plumb loco," he told himself, trudging to the water trough in the failing daylight.

He filled a wash pan with water and put his clothes in to soak with the bar of lye. Passing time, he glanced toward the cabin, its darkened windows and tightly closed doors. When he saw the house, he let out a whispering sigh. "There's a woman in there who needs my help," he said quietly, remembering the swelling and the bruises on Jane's face. "I'm probably diggin' my own grave, but I'm gonna help her out of a fix if I can."

He hung up his clothes to dry and walked to the cookshack. Unfriendly stares greeted him when he came in, and he judged the men had been talking about him. Clay Weeks sat across from Billy, watching Dan from underneath his hat brim. Dan took a plate and filled it with beefsteak and biscuits, determined to eat a good meal in spite of the looks everyone gave him. In just a couple of days, if every-thing went according to plan, he and Jane would be eating on the run, watching their backtrail as they pushed their horses to their limits.

When Dan settled down at the table to eat, he was nagged by the sensation that the three men seated around him had already talked about putting a bullet in him when the time was right. Dan guessed they were only waiting for him to finish the corral fence before they made a move against him. It might have been nothing more than his imagination, but he sensed their intentions while he ate his supper. Something had changed and there was no mis-taking it.

Clay must have told the others that it wouldn't be smart to let an outsider ride off with the knowledge that stolen cattle were being driven to the ranch. I'll have to be extra careful from now on, Dan thought as he chewed a mouthful of steak. Make damn sure I don't turn my back on any of them.

After supper Dan walked down to the wind-mill to pick up his clean clothes, finding them almost dry in a warm summer breeze. Beneath a sky full of bright stars he ambled back to the bunkhouse with his laundry, as tired as he could ever remember after the day's dig-ging. He found himself alone in the bunkhouse while he put his clothing away.

Dan pulled off his boots and stretched out on his bunk to think things through. Just two more days and the herd would arrive. Until the postholes were dug and the fence erected, Dan had to figure that he was safe from a drygulcher's bullet, since none of the others wanted any part of the fence-building chores. Before that corral is finished, he thought, I've got to get my hands on some ammunition for my guns.

Later, he heard boots on the hardpan outside the bunkhouse and he pretended to be asleep. His gunbelt hung beside him on the headboard of his bunk, within easy reach . . . if he had enough time to make a grab for it. He lay still, breathing slowly, as the three men clumped into the room. The cowboys went to their beds without speaking.

He ate breakfast early, before Cookie took the first pan of biscuits from the oven, to be by himself. He'd slept lightly, and his dreams were terrible things . . . visions of a man with a gun slipping up behind him, then a loud explosion that woke him up with a start.

Cookie slammed the pan of biscuits on the table near Dan's elbow, startling Dan from his recollections of the dream.

"They're done," Cookie said. "Salt pork's

on the sideboard and the coffee's ready, so help yourself." Cookie started away from the table, then hesitated and looked at Dan. "How's that corral comin'?" he asked.

"Slow," Dan replied. "Hit some blue flint yesterday. Clay said the herd will be here tomorrow. Sure hope I can get it finished by then."

Cookie nodded thoughtfully. He glanced to the doorway to be sure they were alone. "You watch that Clay Weeks," he said quietly. "He's one mean hombre and he ain't taken a shine to you. Said it wasn't smart to let some outsider go to work on the place. Said he aimed to talk to Jake about it. If there's an hombre on this ranch who's as tough as Jake Logan, it's Clay. I'd watch my backside when I was around that Clay if'n I was you."

Dan stuck a warm biscuit in his mouth. "I'm obliged for the warning, Cookie," he said, chewing, "but there's no reason for that gent to worry about me. Soon as Jake pays me for that fence, I'm headed for New Mexico Territory. Clay's got a burr under his saddle over nothin'. Jake too, he's worried that I'm bein' friendly with his wife, but there ain't no call for that. I ain't in the market for a woman anyhow. Where I'm headed, a woman would only get in the way.

"Besides, I'm sworn to be a bachelor the

rest of my life. When a man hooks up with a woman, he has to take regular baths an' look presentable all the time. That just ain't my natural way of doin' things."

The cook chuckled, like he understood, as he headed back to his kitchen. "You've got the right notion in your head about women," he said over his shoulder. "They're a damn nuisance, most times."

Dan finished his breakfast in silence, hoping the things he told Cookie would reach Clay Weeks. He needed to reassure the men who worked for Jake that he would leave this part of the country with his mouth shut.

If they allowed him to ride off unmolested, his plan was that he would camp in the hills until he saw the dust from the herd moving toward the Mexican border. When it got dark, he would slip back to the ranch and take care of Billy any way he could. Then he and Jane would make their break toward Fort Stockton with at least a couple of days' head start.

He left the cookshack just as the three cowboys came from the bunkhouse. Dan waved and started toward the unfinished digging at a leisurely gait, as though he didn't have a worry in the world. To keep from arousing further suspicion, he had left his gun hanging at the head of his bunk.

He found his tools where he'd left them,

but he noticed a small canvas bag beside the shovel, which hadn't been there the day before. He bent down to examine the bag, opening the drawstring around the mouth. When he saw what was inside, he glanced toward the house and smiled. His hand closed around two paper cartons. One contained shells for a Winchester rimfire. The other box held centerfire cartridges for his Colt. 44. Jane had done exactly as he had asked.

He hid the sack of ammunition near a tree trunk. He felt somewhat better as he lifted the rock bar and began a new posthole. He was ready now if trouble started ahead of schedule.

Chapter 11

Tom was in a surly mood. He'd been assigned the chore of helping Dan finish the corral fence, chopping notches in the posts for the rails, then helping to tie the rails off with smooth wire. The pen was close to completion. Jake said the herd would be there before it got dark. For two miserable days Dan had hurried to finish the fence. The pile of cedar poles had been just enough to build a pair of rails between the posts, with none to spare. By midafternoon they were nearly done with the last section of fence. Since early morning, Tom had said hardly a word to Dan, boiling mad over having to perform the task at Jake's insistence.

The day before, Clay Weeks had ridden off to help with the herd, taking one worry from Dan's mind for the present. Dan was sure that it was Clay's idea to put a bullet in Dan when the herd came in, most likely when Dan tried to ride away from the ranch with money in his pocket.

Dan hadn't seen Jane at all since the night they met at the corrals. She and Jake stayed in the cabin during the day, and Dan would not risk getting close to the house after dark. Now, with plenty of shells for both guns, he was as ready as he ever would be to take Jane westward. Lots of other things had to work just right when he came back for her, but those were things he was prepared for. And he would have the advantage of surprise, slipping back unnoticed after the herd pulled out.

"That's the last one," Dan said, standing back to admire his work when the last rail was tied to a post. It was a crude two-rail fence, but it would hold cattle worn down by days on the trail. If Dan was guessing right, it would require less than two days to alter the brands on two hundred head, which meant he'd have two days to spend out in the hills, waiting for the men and the cattle to depart. So many cows would send up a pall of dust that could be seen for miles, announcing that the time had come for Dan to make his move against Billy. It was the only risky part of the undertaking, coming back at night to get the jump on Billy and tie him up so he couldn't follow them.

Tom made a sour face and dusted off his hands. "Wasn't my damn job in the first place," he growled unhappily. "Jake oughta knowed better'n to put me on a fencin' crew. I was hired to watch the place and lend a hand if there was any problems. Damn sure wasn't hired to build no goddamn fence."

"It's done," Dan said. "Means I can head west, toward them big Guadalupe Mountains, soon as Jake pays me. At ten a month, the way I've got it figured, he owes me mightn' near five dollars." Dan wiped the sweat from his brow. "I'm headed for the house to draw my wages."

Dan ambled toward the cabin, glancing at the horizon to the north where the herd was expected. He found no dust sign.

When he neared the porch, the dog bristled and growled.

"Mister Logan!" he cried, cupping his hands. "I'm done with that fence and I'm ready to pull out!"

He wondered if he might catch a glimpse of Jane when the door opened. But when Jake came out, scowling, there was only darkness behind him until he closed the door. Jake looked at the fence and shook his head.

"It's standin' up," he said, then he looked at Dan. "You aimin' to leave before supper? You got one more free feed comin', and you can stay the night if you take the notion."

Dan wagged his head. "No thanks, boss. I've got this itch to see that New Mexico Territory. I'll be ridin' out as soon as I draw my wages and saddle my buckskin."

Jake pierced him with narrowed eyes. "How much you figure I owe you, Mister Smith?"

Dan shrugged. "Half a month's pay would be fair enough," he answered. "I swear that's the hardest rock in all of Texas out yonder. An' I dug them holes deep, just like you wanted."

Jake nodded once. "Five's fair. Wait here and I'll get you your money." He went back inside and closed the door, leaving Dan alone with his thoughts.

Dan had been worried about Clay Weeks, but since Dan had finished with the fence before Clay got back with the herd, there was a good chance that he would get clear of the ranch without any difficulty. Unless Billy intended to handle the chore. Dan knew he would have to be very careful riding away from this place, keeping an eye on Billy.

The cabin door opened. Jake stalked out with a murderous gleam in his eye, making Dan wonder what Jake was about to do. Dan had gone to work on the fence without his gun and he was defenseless.

Jake walked up to Dan and held out his left hand. Dan glimpsed silver coins between Jake's fingers. Dan took the money . . . five silver dollars, but when he looked down to count it, he saw the gleam of another kind of metal in Jake's right hand. Jake drew his revolver and stuck the cold iron muzzle against Dan's shirtfront.

"Pay real close attention to what I'm about to say," Jake snarled, jutting his jaw, gritting his teeth, leaning closer to Dan's face. "You get on that buckskin and ride hard. Don't ever show yourself 'round here again, and don't open your damn mouth about this place to anybody. You forget that you ever saw this ranch! Ride plumb to New Mexico before you look over your shoulder, and maybe you'll live to a ripe old age. You understand me, cowboy?"

Jake nudged the gun barrel deeper into Dan's belly. His eyes had become angry slits.

Dan raised his hands helplessly. "You've got nothin' to worry about from me, boss," he said quickly, backing away from the feel of the gun. "I'm headed out and I won't be back in your eyesight again. That's a promise, Mister Logan."

Jake grunted. He seemed satisfied and lowered his pistol.

Dan backed away a few steps more. "I'll be gone soon as I get saddled. No call to wave that gun under my nose again. I know when I ain't wanted."

Dan wheeled around and started walking

briskly for the bunkhouse with the money jingling in his fist. He could feel Jake's stare as he hurried across the ranch yard.

He entered the bunkhouse. Billy was nowhere in sight. Tom had gone to the cookshack, and for the time being, Dan found himself alone.

Pulling his war bag from its peg, he fastened his gunbelt around his waist and took his booted rifle from underneath the bunk. The boxes of ammunition were nestled at the bottom of the bag, wrapped in a clean shirt. With everything he owned, he crept to the bunkhouse door and took a cautious look around before he stepped outside. Billy's absence puzzled him, but he continued over to the corral and took his bridle into the pen to catch his horse. Buck nickered softly when Dan came over to the horse.

He slipped the bit into the gelding's mouth and led it over to the fence where the saddles were kept. Placing worn saddle blankets over Buck's withers, then his old saddle, he noticed that one more saddle was missing from the top fence rail. When he swung a glance over his shoulder, he noticed Billy's big gray gelding was missing from the pen.

As soon as he was sure no one was watching him, he booted his rifle below a stirrup leather and then removed a handful of shells from his war bag. Seven cartridges rattled into the loading gate of the Winchester. He worked the lever and sent one into the firing chamber, then lowered the hammer carefully with his thumb. Before he hung the war bag from his saddlehorn, he added two shells to his Colt and snugged it back in its holster. After making sure the saddle was cinched tight around the buckskin's belly, he led the animal to the gate and opened it.

With the gate secured behind him, Dan mounted and heeled the horse away from the corrals. The sounds of hoofbeats brought Tom to the back door of the cookshack. Dan gave the cowboy a friendly wave. Tom simply glared at him, with the beginnings of a grin on his face. The grin puzzled Dan right at first, though he kept the buckskin moving at a trot past the newly finished corral. Lastly, before Dan kicked the gelding to a lope away from the ranch, he swung a look toward the cabin and found the windows dark.

With a sigh of relief he urged Buck to a gallop across a flat that was west of the house, aiming for a stand of live oaks. Some of the tension he felt earlier flowed out of him as he neared the trees. He had made it safely away from a rustler's roost without dodging a single bullet. It had been a close call when Jake stuck his gun in Dan's belly but Jake had only meant to scare him out of the country. If Clay had talked to Jake about silencing Dan permanently, the argument had not worked.

He reached the live oaks and slowed his horse when he was deep inside the grove. Moving at a trot now, he cast a look back to be sure he wasn't followed. Off in the distance, he saw Tom lounging against the back door of the cookshack with his face turned in Dan's direction.

As Dan rode to the edge of the thicket, a gunshot rang out and a whisper of hot air went past his cheek. The buckskin shied from the sound, almost toppling Dan from his saddle until his right hand found the saddlehorn. The shot had come from the south, very close to the spot where Dan held his horse in check now. Someone had been waiting to ambush him and he knew at once that the drygulcher was Billy.

Dan swung his gelding back into the trees and drummed his heels into the horse's ribs. He'd forgotten to put on his spurs in his haste to get away from the ranch, but Buck needed no urging with the echo of the gunshot still ringing in the live oak grove. Buck gave a powerful lunge and bounded among the tree trunks while Dan's hand clawed for his .44/.40. When the gun filled Dan's fist, he swung back in the saddle and tried to find a target among the dense shadows below the limbs.

Another gunshot banged to Dan's right and a slug sizzled through the oak leaves about his head, cracking dully into a limb somewhere behind him. Dan caught a brief glimpse of a yellow muzzle flash in the dark forest, but with the buckskin lunging underneath him he couldn't steady his Colt for a shot. The horse's hooves thundered in the following silence. Every muscle in Dan's body was tensed for the next shot from the bushwhacker. . . . He hunkered down over the horse's neck to present as small a target as possible while the buckskin galloped at full speed through the trees, back in the direction of the ranch.

When he reached the eastern edge of the thicket Dan jerked back on the reins and brought his horse to a sliding halt. He listened for the sounds of a pursuing horseman and heard nothing. Dan's nerves were so rattled by the gunshots that for a moment he couldn't think clearly. He looked north, and saw empty grassland stretching to a group of low hills. Reining that way, he drummed the buckskin's sides and sent it into a full gallop away from the live oaks. The horse lengthened its strides and stretched out at a pounding run, its black mane flying in Dan's face as it reached top speed. Dan aimed a look backward. At first he saw nothing, then a shadow moved deep inside the thicket and the shadow became the outline of a horse and rider, coming after Dan at a run.

Dan leaned over the buckskin's neck without trying to aim at his pursuer. The distance was too great for any accuracy and only a lucky shot would find its mark now. Pounding his heels into the horse's ribs, he rode toward the hills, glancing back when he dared, watching for gopherholes in the buckskin's path that might bring a sudden end to the horse race. For half a minute he gave the gelding its head and scanned the hills in front of him.

When he reached the first low hill he swung a look over his shoulder. More than a quarter of a mile behind, he saw a gray gelding galloping after him, and he quickly recognized its rider. Billy rode hard along Dan's tracks. Sunlight glinted off the pistol he held in his hand.

"Give me all you've got, Buck!" Dan shouted, sending the horse up the gentle slope at an all-out run. Dan clung to the butt of his pistol so tightly that his palm had begun to ache. The gelding bounded up the slope and then across the hilltop. As Dan glanced backward, a puff of gunsmoke billowed from Billy's pistol, and a fraction later he heard the crack of the shot. Three more long strides by the buckskin carried Dan out of sight over the top of the hill. Below, a winding ravine thick with summer-dry grass turned westward, the direction Dan wanted to travel. The gelding raced to the bottom of the hill and responded to the pressure of the reins when Dan swung it into the ravine. The clatter of galloping hoofbeats changed when Buck crossed the rocky bottom of the gully. Once, the horse stumbled and Dan feared they might go tumbling to the floor of the ravine, but the gelding caught itself quickly and regained its long running strides between the walls of the wash.

Buck had begun to gasp for air. Wind whistled through his muzzle and the sound was a warning that the chase would end soon. Dan had no way to judge the stamina of the gray gelding behind him and it was only a guess that Buck could keep running long enough to outlast the horse Billy rode. Down the length of the ravine, Buck's breathing grew louder, forcing Dan to begin a search for a place offering good defenses for the moment when the chase was finally over.

At a turn in the dry wash, Dan found what he was looking for. On the rim above the ravine sat a tiny knot of live oaks and mesquite where a gunman, and a horse, would be hidden from the bottom of the wash. Dan slowed the buckskin when he neared the trees, looking for a way to ride up the bank. Just past the trees, the bank had a more gradual slope and it was here that Dan turned his horse to begin the climb.

Buck was puffing for wind by the time they reached the top. Dan rode into the trees and dropped from his saddle to draw the rifle from its boot and find a firing position. Glancing back up the draw he saw no dust sign, and when Dan stepped to the edge of the grove, he heard no hoofbeats.

"He turned back," Dan gasped, squinting in the late-day heat haze to be sure his eyes weren't playing tricks on him. "His gray played out back there someplace . . . couldn't stay up with Buck all that distance." Buck's stamina had been one reason why Dan selected the gelding a few years back. He had bought the horse below Aquila from a man who raised thoroughbred stock and sold them to the cavalry. It had proven to be a wise choice many times in the past, when the big buckskin carried Dan away from tight spots and a disagreement or two.

He watched the ravine a while longer, until it was plain that no one followed him now. Cradling the Winchester in the crook of an arm, he walked back to his groundhitched gelding and patted him softly on the neck. "You saved my skin this time, ol' hoss," he said, mounting slowly, still looking back at the draw. "With some of this silver I've got jinglin' in my pockets, I'll buy you a sack of grain at the next town we come across."

Reining westward, he let the horse move at a walk toward the setting sun. Although Dan's nerves were still raw-edged from the close brush with Billy Cole, he felt a little better now. Resting the rifle against his thigh, he pushed west across rolling hills and dry caliche flats to put as much distance as he could between himself and Billy before dark. He checked his backtrail often.

The sun became a crimson ball on the horizon. Deepening purple shadows fell away from the trees and brush dotting the hillsides. Night birds called to each other in the twilight, fluttering from the buckskin's path. Dan crossed more miles of empty land until dusk became dark. Stars sprinkled the sky as he looked for a camp.

An hour later, crossing a starlit valley, Dan found a tiny pocket of rainwater at the bottom of a rocky basin. He let the horse drink its fill, then he rode to a clump of mesquites and swung down. When the gelding was unsaddled and hobbled on good grass, he spread his bedroll at the edge of the mesquite thicket and sat down to rest. He knew he couldn't risk a fire. There was a chance that Billy was still trailing him.

Gazing up at the stars, he thought about the attempt on his life. It had been an ill wind that had blown him toward the Logan ranch that day, and it all had come about because his belly was as empty as his pockets. All he'd wanted was a few square meals and a job. Instead, he'd ridden headlong into a nest of killers and cattle thieves, and had his conscience put to the test when he found that a woman was being held against her will at the ranch. Only a few hours ago, somebody had tried to kill him. Staring at the sky, he wondered why things had gotten so all-fired complicated.

Chapter 12

On a wooded hill miles to the south of the ranch, Dan studied what was going on inside the corrals. Dust boiled into a cloudless sky above the pens. Men resembling tiny ants roped the cattle and pulled them to a branding fire. This was the second day of branding. Yesterday, Dan hadn't been willing to risk riding close enough to see what was going on, still watchful in case Billy was riding the hills west of the ranch.

Now he saw that there were five new cowhands among the men working the branding irons. Adding Jake to the tally, nine men moved in and out of the pens during the morning, though they were only little dots from Dan's vantage point.

All morning, he had pondered how he would approach the bunkhouse after Jake and his men had driven out the herd. It was safest to wait until Billy would be asleep, sometime after midnight. Making a quiet approach to the bunkhouse promised to be the most difficult task because of the risk of the dog barking.

Resting in the shade of an oak, Dan considered the fateful action he was about to take. If I had any sense, he thought, I'd keep riding west with this hard-earned money and forget about what was happening here.

He took a deep breath and sighed. He knew he couldn't simply forget about what Jake was doing to Jane. "I'm caught like a pig stuck under a gate," he told himself. "I can't just ride off. Couldn't live with myself if I did."

He turned for his horse and mounted, casting a final look at the distant corrals.

They'll pull out soon, he thought. I'll see the dust.

He swung the buckskin off the hilltop and headed west, to be in a better position to slip up on the bunkhouse as soon as it got dark. Riding a wide circle around the ranch, keeping off the skyline while moving slowly so he wouldn't send a telltale dust sign into the air, he thought about the moment when he crept up on Billy. If the gunman woke up before he could knock him out cold, he would be forced to use his gun.

I've never killed a man before, he thought.

A few years back, while riding fence for a rancher named Dave Watkins, he'd had to shoot his way out of a tight spot when he rode up on two men who were cutting a handful of steers from Watkins's herd. Both men came out with guns, and Dan answered their fire almost before he had time to think about the jam he was in. One rustler tumbled from his saddle with a shoulder wound while the other hightailed it without the bunch of steers. Dan's first bullet had dropped the outlaw and that had apparently been enough to convince the other gent that he wanted no part of a gunfight with Dan.

But I never killed nobody, he thought again, wondering if he could when the chips were down. A few days earlier, he'd been sure he could kill Jake Logan. But as the thought tumbled around inside Dan's head, he found himself nagged by little doubts. He had promised Jane that a bullet would stop Jake if he came after her, and that promise continued to echo through his thoughts as he made the circle around the ranch.

Just past noon, while Dan rested in the shade of an oak grove, he looked up and saw dust boiling into the sky. Dan came to his feet to study the dust cloud. "They're pulling out," he said softly. "I'll get my chance tonight."

He walked to the edge of the thicket and watched the dust move slowly southward. A worried frown pinched Dan's features, for he knew he was spending his last peaceful afternoon for many days to come.

Crickets were chirping all around him. Pale moonlight bathed the open stretches between the trees. Creeping toward the darkened bunkhouse on the balls of his feet, he made a soundless approach from the northeast. His buckskin was tied in a stand of trees better than a quarter mile from the ranch. He'd hung his spurs on his saddle horn and drawn his Colt. With his nerves raw-edged, he crept to the north wall of the bunkhouse and paused to listen for Billy's snoring. He could hear it plainly through the thin plank wall, and when he heard the sound, some of the tension left him.

The corrals were empty. Only three horses remained in the pen where the geldings were kept. Billy's big gray rested hipshot near the fence, head lowered, swishing its tail now and then.

Dan looked up at the stars, guessing that it was almost midnight now. Then he moved quietly toward the back of the cookshack to find a firewood club to use on Billy. Dan tiptoed across fresh wagon tracks where Cookie had driven away with the chuck for the men pushing the herd. If the dog did not bark and awaken Billy, everything would work the way Dan wanted.

At the stack of firewood behind the cook-shack he selected a green mesquite limb that he judged had just the right heft to it. With his pistol in one hand and the club in the other, he started for the bunkhouse door with his heart racing.

He was forced to cross a piece of open ground to reach the bunkhouse door. Pausing, Dan glanced over his shoulder at the cabin's dark windows, wondering if Jane was awake . . . perhaps watching now behind one of the curtains, ready for the moment when Dan called to her.

Dan's breathing quickened. His palms were damp around the gun and the stick of fire-wood. He started forward again, inching his way across the barren, moonlit ground, lis-tening to the beat of his heart.

A sudden noise made him freeze in mid-stride. The dog began to bark angrily from the cabin porch, and the sound was like a roll of thunder intruding upon the night silence. Every muscle in Dan's body went rigid. . . . He knew the dog would wake Billy and bring him scrambling outside with a gun. Dan was caught in an open stretch between the bunk-house and the cookshack, making a perfect target in the moonlight with no place to run if Billy were quick to reach the bunkhouse door.

Dan took off in a lumbering run for the cookshack, glancing over his shoulder as he ran. Boots thumping over the hardpan, he raced blindly for a dark corner of the building, watching for Billy to emerge from the bunkhouse before Dan could reach the safety of the corner.

A shadow moved near the doorway, then a gun exploded. A flash of bright light flickered, revealing Billy's face and shoulders before the muzzleflash faded. A stab of white-hot pain entered Dan's left elbow, knocking the mesquite limb from his grasp. Dan stumbled and fell face-first on the hard caliche, sliding forward on his chest with dust and sand suddenly filling his eyes and mouth.

Another gunshot rocked the brief silence. A bullet plowed a furrow near Dan's face, making a hissing noise past his right ear. Things were happening before Dan could clear his addled brain, and the pain in his elbow was like a raging fire. Dan whirled over on his back, swinging his gun in the direction of the bunkhouse. But his eyes were full of gritty particles and he discovered that he was almost blind.

Billy's pistol roared again. A speeding lead slug whispered above Dan's head and whacked into the wall of the cookshack. Dan blinked furiously, trying to clear his vision while he cocked his .44/.40. With his eyes blurred by dust and tears, he found a dim shape near the bunkhouse steps and pulled the trigger. The Colt thundered in his hand and spat a finger of yellow flame. The bang of the gun was deafening. Dan's ears were ringing, and at first, he couldn't be sure of the next sound he heard.

He sat up, and the movement sent a new shock of pain up his wounded arm that brought an involuntary cry from Dan's throat. He aimed his Colt at the darkness, briefly blinded by its muzzleflash and the particles in his eyes from his fall, all the while wondering if this was his last moment on earth. If Billy fired again, only a piece of luck would keep the gunman's aim from finding him a sitting target in the moonlight.

An eerie silence followed. Dan pierced the black shadows near the bunkhouse steps, thumbing back the hammer on his Colt for a shot before he found anything to shoot at. Where was Billy? The steps leading into the bunkhouse showed plainly. Had the gunman jumped back inside, even now aiming around the door frame for a shot that couldn't miss at this range?

Then Dan heard a soft groan coming from a shadow below the eaves of the bunkhouse. With his heart racing, wincing from the waves of pain in his elbow, Dan scrambled to his feet, covering the front of the building with his gun. Panting, his head reeling with a sick dizziness that knotted his stomach, his injured arm dangling uselessly at his side, he staggered toward the shadows where he heard the groan. Another cautious step and he felt a trickle of warm blood run down his shirtsleeve. Gasping for air and shaking his head to clear it, he moved closer to the bunkhouse on unsteady legs, trying to see what lay hidden in the shadows.

He heard the groan again and he halted. Peering down, he saw a body lying against the wall. Behind him, off in the distance, he could hear the dog barking savagely. But Dan ignored everything else and took another careful step toward Billy, covering him with the Colt, his finger tightened around the trigger.

Billy's gun lay a few feet from his outstretched hand, and when Dan saw it, he let out a ragged breath and hurried over to it on reeling legs. When his boot was pressed over the barrel of the pistol, Dan let out a sigh and allowed his trigger finger to relax. Billy rested against the bunkhouse wall, groaning softly each time he took a breath. In the darkness, Dan couldn't see where his bullet had struck Billy, but right then all that mattered was keeping Billy's gun where it was now, underneath the sole of Dan's boot.

With the danger past, Dan became aware again of the throbbing pain that went from his elbow to his shoulder. Waiting until he could catch his breath and steady his legs a bit more, he simply stood a few yards away from Billy with his gun aimed down.

Behind him, the dog fell silent. Then running footsteps came toward the bunkhouse. Dan risked a look over his shoulder. Jane ran toward him across the pale caliche, her hair flying behind her. He looked back down at Billy. The boiling sickness in his belly grew worse, and he worried that his legs might give way. He took his boot off Billy's gun and bent down slowly to pick it up. Waves of nausea washed over him before he could stick the warm pistol in the waistband of his denims.

Jane ran up to him and he turned to look at her, hoping he wouldn't fall flat on his face when the dizziness swirled around in his skull.

"Dan!" she cried, before she reached his side. "I heard the shots. . . . What happened?"

Dan pointed to Billy with the barrel of his gun. "Had to shoot him," Dan said around clenched teeth, for now the pain shot up his arm like bolts of lightning. "Can't tell how bad it is. He got me in the arm. I'm gonna need some bandages. I can feel the blood runnin' down my sleeve and it hurts like hell."

Jane bent down to examine his left arm,

touching his shirtsleeve lightly, then he heard her gasp.

"There's a lot of blood," she whispered. "Come to the house so I can light a lantern. I can clean the wound and bandage it tight."

Dan shook his head. "Not just yet . . . not till I'm sure this owlhoot ain't got any more fight left in him." He walked closer to Billy and bent down to see where his bullet had struck. Billy still groaned softly, barely conscious it seemed. His hat lay a few feet beyond his head, and it was then that Dan saw the dark bloodstain on the ground below Billy's ear. Fighting waves of nausea, Dan went down on one knee for a closer look.

A bloody gash was open across Billy's forehead. Dan's slug had caught him with a glancing path above his right eye. "It's just a flesh wound," Dan said. "We'll have to tie him up. Appears he's just stunned right now. Can't take any chances, Jane. Get me a piece of rope. You'll have to help me. My left arm is plumb useless . . . can't hardly move it. When Billy wakes up, he'll come after us unless we tie him down real tight."

He heard the woman trot away. His head was reeling. He sat down on the ground beside Billy, avoiding any movement of his injured arm until he was forced to bend it gently across his lap. He put his Colt down and tenderly fingered the bullet wound just below his elbow. There was an exit wound at the top of his forearm. At least he wouldn't have to have the bullet removed from his arm. It seemed small consolation just then, hurting the way he was. The blood loss would weaken him considerably, at a time when he needed all his strength for the breakneck ride toward Fort Stockton.

Even seated on the ground, he was feeling dizzy. There was much to be done and he'd have to do it one-handed. Jane's horse had to be saddled, after Billy was tied up. And it was a quarter-mile walk to his buckskin, too far for a man on wobbly legs. Adding things up, he knew that he faced the roughest ride of his life. The damaged elbow would only hurt worse, jostled by the gait of a horse.

On the other side of things, Billy was out of the fight and Dan's gun hand was still usable. He wouldn't be able to fire the rifle, as it required two good arms. Still, things could be worse, he reasoned.

Jane ran up to him with a length of rope. In the pale moonlight Dan could see the worry on her face. Dan rolled up on his knees, forcing his mind away from fresh jolts of pain when he moved his arm. "Help me," he whispered, lifting one of Billy's hands to his stomach, then the other. "Tie one end of that rope around his wrists. Then we'll tie his feet, so he can't walk."

Jane surprised him then. He wasn't expecting a gentle kiss on his left cheek.

"I didn't think you'd come back," she said softly. "I wouldn't have blamed you if you hadn't."

He grinned in spite of the throbbing pain. "I gave you my word," he answered quietly.

Chapter 13

He watched her face in the lantern glow as she tied strips of bedsheet around his elbow after his wounds were washed and covered with the foul-smelling oil she had applied to Bob Huffman's injury. The lantern hissed softly on the table beside her, its soft light illuminating her pretty green eyes and smooth skin. The bruises on her face were still there, dark reminders of her husband's cruelty.

"There," she said, finished with the last knot in the bandages. "Now I'll make a sling. Can you bend your arm?"

"A little," he answered, complying with her request very slowly, feeling renewed stabs of pain with even the slightest movement.

She took a larger piece of cloth and gently fashioned a sling underneath his forearm, then tied the ends behind his neck.

"We better get moving," he said, standing up a little unsteadily at first. "Got to get a horse saddled for you. There's a chestnut gelding down at the pens that looks like he can run."

"I can do it," Jane replied as she went to a corner of the room to pick up an old carpetbag valise. He watched her hurry over to a bullhide chair. She took a gunbelt from the back of the chair and quickly strapped it around her waist. Dan noticed a small pocket-model Colt .41 caliber in the holster.

"Can you use a gun?" he asked.

A smile flashed briefly across her face. "Of course I can," she replied. Her hand fell to the pistol and she took it out, thumbing open the loading gate while she glanced at the brass cartridges in the cylinder before she closed it. She handled the gun expertly, as though she'd done it many times before. When the pistol was back in its holster, she looked at Dan again. "You've gotten the impression that I'm helpless, Dan," she said evenly, as a strange look came to her eyes. "I can only guess that you've never been to Hell's Half Acre in Fort Worth. Helpless women don't last very long in that part of town. You won't have to take care of me — I'll be right there beside you every step of the way." She carried her valise to the front door, where she paused and looked Dan squarely in the eye. "And if Jake finds us before we get where we're going, I'll show you how well I can shoot.

I'll kill Jake before I let him bring me back to this place!"

Even with the pain throbbing in his arm, Dan chuckled. "Had you figured for a tough little lady all along," he said. "Let's get that horse saddled, and I'll check on those ropes around Billy. We're gonna make it out of here, you an' me. A time or two I got worried that we'd have our hands full if Jake an' some of his men caught up to us. But now I ain't so worried. Let's get a move on."

He followed Jane out of the cabin. He was puzzled when she stood on the porch, staring back inside before she closed the door.

"This is the last time I'll see this prison," she said in a hoarse whisper. "Goodbye, Jake! I'll see you in hell if you come after me!"

She slammed the door and hurried down the steps. Dan followed in her footsteps, wincing as each footfall reached his bad arm. They crossed the barren hardpan to the corral, where Jane took down a bridle and then hurried to the corral gate to catch her horse.

A thought occurred to Dan when his gaze wandered to Billy's saddle on the top fence rail. He reached in his pocket and opened his Barlow knife, then cut the cinch strap in half and watched it fall to the ground. "Just in case he gets himself loose," Dan said softly.

Jane trotted out the gate, leading the chestnut. She tied it to the fence and swung the remaining saddle over its withers. It surprised Dan that she knew her way around horses. She pulled the latigo like a seasoned cowboy.

"I'll check on Billy," he said, turning for the bunkhouse. His legs worked better now, although the pain in his arm was no less. He crossed to the eave where they'd left Billy. The gunman was still trussed up like a hog at butchering time, and he appeared to be asleep.

Dan heard Jane trot her horse over to the bunkhouse. "Get up behind me, Dan," she said. Her valise was hanging from her saddlehorn and the climb up behind her would be difficult for a man with just one good arm.

"Ain't rightly sure I can," he replied doubtfully.

Jane swung down, landing on both feet beside him. "I'll help you up first and I'll ride behind you," she said.

He grabbed the pommel with his right hand and made a painful pull over the saddle. Before he was settled against the cantle, Jane swung up behind him and then laced her arms around his waist, carefully avoiding his injured arm with her hand.

Dan reined the chestnut away from the bunkhouse and urged the horse to a walk. His elbow throbbed with the horse's gait and he took a deep breath, knowing he faced days of intense pain in a saddle before this ride was over.

Just then, Jane snuggled her cheek against his neck, making him forget the pain briefly. The feel of her arms around him was good too, and for a time he forgot about his elbow, enjoying the woman's nearness.

"I knew I was right about you," she whispered in his ear, her gentle breath tickling him so he shivered. "I knew the first time I saw you that you weren't like the others. You're a brave man, Dan Willis. I still don't know why you are helping me, but it doesn't matter what your reasons are. I want you to know I'm very grateful for what you're doing." She tightened her arms around his waist, then she kissed him lightly again. Just a peck on the cheek.

He felt a blush rise in his cheeks. In the dark, she wouldn't be aware of his embarrassment. Guiding the chestnut toward the spot where he'd tied the buckskin, he felt a certain amount of satisfaction. Though his elbow pained him greatly, they were leaving the Logan ranch as he'd promised Jane they would. Dangerous miles lay before them, but Dan told himself that they would make it. Somehow.

Buck nickered when the chestnut came close. Dan reined over to the trees where his horse was hidden. Almost before he pulled the chestnut to a halt, Jane jumped off the horse's rump, landing gracefully beside the left stirrup.

"I'll help you down," she said.

"I can manage," he argued, swinging a leg over the cantle with great care. His arm throbbed when he moved it at all. A dull, constant ache had settled around his elbow. When his feet touched the ground, he examined his bandage in the moon glow. Blood had seeped through, darkening the bedsheet.

He mounted Buck with some difficulty and took a deep breath, steeling himself for the jolting ride. "We'll have to ride slow for a spell," he told her. "This arm is killin' me when I move it."

He noticed Jane opening her valise, then she urged her horse alongside Buck and handed Dan a pint bottle of whiskey. "Drink some of this," she said. "It'll soften the hurt some."

He took the bottle and stared at it. "I make it a practice to leave this stuff alone," he said. "But I reckon these are special circumstances."

He took a small swallow and made a face when the burn scalded the inside of his mouth.

The fire went down his throat and spread through his belly. He forced himself to take another drink, for it seemed that the whiskey had an immediate effect on the ache in his arm.

Buck fidgeted underneath him and he gave the pint back to Jane. "Let's put some miles behind us," he said, swinging his horse away from the trees.

At a walk, his bad arm swayed against his ribcage, sending tiny rushes of pain up to his shoulder. He heeled the buckskin and sent it to a slow trot, standing in his stirrups to soften the pounding of a faster pace. Standing eased the pain almost at once. He could travel like this for miles. Jane rode up beside him and he saw a question on her face. "I can ride," he said.

Jane smiled, leaning out of her saddle to touch his good arm. "Let me know when you need to stop and rest," she said, above the rattle of iron horseshoes.

He nodded. Her touch reminded him of the kisses she had given him, and the recollection brought a thrill of excitement to his chest. He wondered if her kisses had been only kindness. He reasoned that it was too soon to judge that sort of thing. They would have time to get to know each other across the miles to Fort Stockton, and beyond. There was a chance that Jane Logan might discover that there was more to Dan than appearances showed.

They rode through the live oaks where Billy had ambushed Dan, and he was reminded of how close he had come to a bullet hole in his back. At least they didn't have to worry about Billy now. Perhaps Lady Luck had decided to favor Dan Willis for a change.

"How's the arm?" Jane asked, riding alongside him so closely that their knees almost touched.

"I'm doin' okay," he replied, glancing down at his bandage. "At least the bleeding's stopped."

They trotted out of the trees, facing the group of grassy hills to the west where Dan had ridden two days earlier to escape Billy's ambush. To test greater speed with his aching arm, he sent the buckskin into a short lope. He soon discovered that at a gallop he could rest against the seat of his saddle without adding any pain to his wound, and he could rest his legs when they tired, after standing in the stirrups.

He expected his wound would fester for a few days, and the festering would be accompanied by fever. A week or more would be needed before proper healing would begin. Facing almost a hundred miles of rough country to reach Fort Stockton, he judged they would make little more than twenty-five miles a day. Maybe less, if they had to spend precious time searching dry country for water for the horses. The canteen tied to his saddle was full, enough to keep them both alive if the land to the west was really dry. But the horses couldn't be pushed without water, and looking for it would delay them unless they found it along the Fort Stockton road.

Entering the hills, they kept their horses in a short lope. As they rode west, with the moon showing the landscape, Dan felt himself relax more and more, rocking gently against the cantle while Buck carried him farther and farther away from the outlaws' den where he'd almost lost his life.

Dawn put them on a barren prairie. Just before sunrise, they encountered a pair of wagon ruts leading westward. The seldom-used road made for easier travel for the horses. Galloping, then walking the animals until they were rested, Dan guessed they had come more than fifteen miles through the hills to reach this flat expanse.

Jane seemed none the worse after the night of hard riding. She rode beside him, looking back now and then to check their backtrail. She rode a horse easily, like an experienced rider, for which Dan was silently grateful.

Should Jake and some of his men catch up to them before they reached a safe place, Dan knew the woman could sit a saddle if there was a chase.

Jane opened her valise and removed a small cloth bundle. She handed Dan a strip of jerky. "Breakfast," she said brightly, as if she'd just given him a platter of bacon and eggs.

He took a bite of the meat and nodded his thanks.

"There's plenty more," she said, taking a piece for herself before she put the bundle away. "I've got some money. We can buy more supplies when we need them."

"Won't be a place where we can buy 'em," he said, remembering the two tiny dots on the surveyor's map. "Just open country till we get to Fort Stockton. We've got three days of hard ridin' ahead of us . . . mostly open range. Water's gonna be our biggest problem, enough water for our horses, if we can find it. A muleskinner back at Mason told me it was dry as a powderkeg out west this time of year. Teamsters haul their own water barrels in late summer so the mules can make it through."

Jane frowned. "I didn't think about water," she said. "What'll we do if we can't find it?"

Dan shook his head. "Ride slow and spare these horses all we can. Travel at night, maybe, when a horse don't sweat so much. I'm new to dry country myself. Where I growed up, water was never a big problem. But don't worry yourself about it. We'll make it. You've got my word on that."

She laughed, and he liked the sound of it.

"I won't ever doubt your word on anything, Dan," she said, still smiling. "You came back for me, just like you said you would. I'm a believer." Then she looked at him strangely in the soft morning sunlight, as if she saw something she hadn't seen before. Her steady gaze started to make him uncomfortable.

Soon the heat began to build. When they galloped their horses, the animals' necks grew wet with lather. A blazing west Texas sun baked the prairie before them. Heat waves began to dance in the distance, creating the illusion of water. A hot wind blew in their faces from the southwest, gaining intensity as the sun climbed higher. Continuing along the faint wagon road, they traveled in silence until noon. As the hours passed, Dan felt a gradual change in the sensation around his elbow. His arm had begun to swell. He felt lightheaded when his horse was at a lope and his face felt hot to the touch.

They rode to a gentle swell in the prairie where scattered mesquite trees offered sparse shade. Dan reined his gelding to a halt and gave Jane a weak grin.

"I could use a rest," he said, easing down from the seat of his saddle, avoiding any movement of his bad arm. A reeling dizziness made him feel faint. He groundhitched Buck, walked slowly to the base of a tree, then lowered himself gently to the dry grass and leaned back against the trunk with his hat tilted over his eyes.

"Are you all right?" Jane asked.

He heard her kneel down beside him. "A mite dizzy just now," he answered softly, "and hotter'n grandma's stove."

The horses grazed hungrily underneath the trees while Jane walked off to look for water. Dan closed his eyes, wondering if he were merely exhausted after a long night's ride without sleep. The swelling in his forearm strained against the bandage, making the ache seem worse. He knew the fever would rob him of strength until it broke.

Water sloshed inside his canteen when Jane returned to the tree. Then she took the hat off his face and pressed a cool damp rag over his forehead.

"Don't waste that water," he warned sleepily. He was drifting off in spite of his efforts to stay awake. The wet cloth felt good against his burning skin, and he finally let go, slipping toward a blanket of fog swirling around his eyes. His last conscious thought was a product of fear. How many hours would pass before Jake Logan began his search for his missing wife? In the foggy condition his brain was in now, he'd lost all track of time.

He awoke with a start. His surroundings were dark. Where was he? Then he saw the sky sprinkled with twinkling stars above him and his mind started to clear.

He worked his right elbow underneath him and pushed up from the ground, blinking. Then he felt a hand touch him on the shoulder.

"Everything's okay," Jane whispered. "You passed out. You've got a bad fever."

Dan shuddered, suddenly cold. Gooseflesh pimpled his skin and his mouth tasted like cotton. "I'm freezin'," he said in a distant voice.

She draped a blanket around his shoulders.

"I took down your bedroll," Jane said, tugging the blanket under his chin. "Drink a little more of this whiskey."

He heard the cork pop out of the bottleneck and smelled the vapors of barley mash below his nose. He took the pint and lifted it to his lips, noticing that he was shivering. A mouthful of bitter whiskey burned down his throat, then another, taking his breath away. "That's the awfulest tastin' stuff in the world," he said when he could get air in his lungs.

Jane wiped his face again with the cool cloth. "We can rest here until morning," she said quietly. "I'll build a fire and boil some coffee."

Dan shook his head quickly. "No fire. If anybody's out here, we don't want them to find us."

Later, after another swallow of whiskey, Jane helped him lie down in the grass. She covered him with the blanket.

"I'll be right here if you need me," she whispered.

Chapter 14

He slept fitfully, awakening often, shivering inside his thin blanket. And each time he awoke, Jane was there, reassuring him with her soft voice, cooling his skin with the damp rag. His arm throbbed with rolling spasms of pain from which sleep was the only escape. As dawn brightened the eastern sky he sat up slowly, painfully, shuddering inside the blanket.

Jane came toward him from the tree where the horses were tied. Worry put tiny crow's feet beside her eyes when she knelt beside him. "You had a rough night," she said gently. "The fever's worse. I cleaned your wound and tied a clean bandage over it while you were asleep. There's a lot of swelling, but I don't know what else to do."

"I'll be okay," Dan said, trying to make the remark sound as convincing as he could. He looked east, where the sun peeked above the horizon. "We've got to be moving. Help me get on my horse. We can't stay here."

Jane was shaking her head before he finished. "You're too weak to ride, Dan," she replied. "You must rest, until your fever breaks."

Dan shook his head. "Too risky. For all we know, Billy has gotten loose from them ropes by now and he's headed after Jake to tell him what happened. Or headed down our tracks . . ."

"You can't sit a saddle," she protested, pressing her hand against his shoulder when he tried to get up.

Dan gave her a look. "I'm a little tougher'n you give me credit for, pretty lady," he said, forcing a grin. "Now help me up."

Her brow furrowed, but she said nothing more and got up to help him to his feet. With slow but steady effort, Dan worked his knees underneath him, then struggled upward and tried to stand steady on uncertain legs. He took a deep breath when a tidal wave of nausea washed through his belly. Tiny pinpoints of light blinked before his eyes. The trees around him tilted crazily and he felt himself falling . . . falling . . . falling with a syrupy slowness.

He was lying down, damp from head to toe. His shirt was stuck to him like a second skin and his denims clung to his legs. Perspiration dripped from his face when he sat up, forming little damp circles on the blanket across his lap. It was then, as his vision cleared, that he noticed the sky darkening with nightfall. Purple shadows fell away from the mesquites. He blinked and shook his head. Had he slept all day?

He glanced toward the horses and found but one. Buck stood hipshot, swishing flies away, half asleep. The chestnut gelding was gone. Gradually a grim message worked its way into Dan's brain: Jane had left him to fend for himself. Although he supposed it was her fear that had made her do it, Dan's heart fell. In vain, he looked at the darkening prairie around the hilltop. The woman had ridden off and he supposed he couldn't blame her much, though he now knew he had misjudged her.

The bottle of whisky lay beside him, and with his mood becoming as dark as the west Texas skies above his head, he pulled the cork with his teeth and took a long, bubbling swallow. The whiskey was as bitter as the realization he faced . . . Jane Logan had gone on without him. The risks he'd taken had not been enough to tie her to this hilltop when she found he was unable to ride. He knew it was fear that made her choice for her, and thinking about it just then, Dan forgave her for leaving him behind.

He rolled up on his knees, limbs trembling with weakness, then got slowly to his feet, steadying himself against the tree trunk with his good arm. His fever had broken and he felt better. He was sure he could ride now, albeit slowly. He picked up his blanket and the pint of whiskey and walked slowly toward his buckskin, damp clothing hugging every angle of his body.

It required a great deal of effort to tie his bedroll behind the saddle with just one hand, but he managed. And when the pint was tucked into his war bag, he loosened the gelding's reins and began the slow, painful climb into his saddle seat. Dusk paled the flat grasslands to the west as he rode out of the mesquite thicket at a walk. He was thinking about Jane as he left the hilltop, his heart heavy with the knowledge that she was gone.

Riding toward the last rays of sunlight brightening the horizon, he wondered where Jane had headed — whether she had continued toward Fort Stockton or gone off in another direction. Maybe she had planned all along to desert him, first chance she got. Doubt and suspicion welled up inside him as he rode along.

A movement caught his eye in the distance. Was it a horse and rider? Could it be Jane, only a few miles ahead of him, heading west along the wagon road?

The outline of a horse and rider seemed closer, growing larger, although the growing darkness prevented him from being sure. Waiting, watching the movement on the prairie before him, he blinked in confusion when it appeared that the horseman was riding in his direction rather than away from him.

Minutes later, he recognized Jane atop the trotting chestnut gelding, and she was riding toward him. The corners of his mouth turned up in an unconscious grin. She was riding back toward the hilltop. Had she changed her mind about leaving him behind?

When she saw him, she kicked her horse to a lope. Dan slowed the buckskin and waited for her. Jane galloped up to him and hauled back on the reins.

"Where are you going?" she asked, urging her horse alongside his, staring into his eyes. "I went looking for water. The canteen was almost empty, and your fever was getting worse. I felt I had to do something." Then she narrowed her eyelids. "Why did you ride off without me?" she asked.

He couldn't look at her right then, averting his gaze. "I figured you went on by yourself . . . when I couldn't sit a horse. I couldn't blame you, if that's what you did."

Jane lifted her chin just a little. "Is that the

sort of person you think I am, Dan Willis?" she asked. "Did you think I'd run out on you?"

For a time, he didn't answer. Then he blurted out the truth. "I guessed you was afraid Jake was coming, and taking care of me was slowing you down."

She leaned out of her saddle. A fierce gleam brightened her eyes. "Then you don't know me very well!" she spat angrily, as if he'd insulted her deeply. "I never ran out on a friend in my life! I was looking for water. This canteen was almost dry!"

"Sorry," he said sheepishly, with a shrug. "I reckon I took things wrong."

"You did," she answered with slightly less heat in her voice, although her eyes still smoldered with green fire. "You risked your life to help me, Dan. I'd never pull out on you when you were in trouble."

He wanted to change the subject as quickly as he could. "It's gettin' dark. My fever broke and I'm feelin' a lot better. Let's cover some country while I can still sit this saddle."

Jane shook her head. "I couldn't find a spring," she said quietly, casting a glance over her shoulder in the direction from which she had come. "Our horses need water. This gelding's flanks are getting drawn. I started back as soon as the sun went down."

171

Dan knew Buck was suffering equally. "We'll spare them some if we travel tonight. Keep your eyes peeled for a stand of trees around a low spot. When the moon comes up, we'll be able to see treetops from a pretty good distance in this flat country." He lifted his reins and prepared to ride off.

Jane reached out to touch his arm. "Believe this, Dan," she began in a soft voice, "that I couldn't ever leave you helpless out here after what you've done for me. I'm not made that way."

He grinned back at her. "I guess I just wasn't thinkin' straight." He heeled the buckskin to a walk and headed west.

Jane fell in beside him. In the failing daylight, she glanced over at his bandaged arm. "How does it feel?" she asked.

"Still hurts," he replied, testing his elbow with a slight movement that sent a prickling pain up his arm. "But I'll make a few miles." He urged the gelding to a short lope.

Galloping, then resting their horses at a walk, they rode into the darkness along the wagon road. Dan had never seen a country so empty. Flat prairie stretched for miles in every direction, broken only by occasional low hills and scattered knots of mesquite and beds of cactus. Here and there, spiked sotol plants reared up from the grasslands like fire-blackened spines against the night sky. A warm wind blew gently in their faces, smelling dry, hinting of dust.

Jane surprised him later on when she asked a question. "Were you ever married, Dan?"

He shook his head. "Never found a woman who could tolerate me," he answered. "Thought I was in love a time or two, but things just didn't work out. I've been a travelin' man most of my life. Most women are lookin' for a man who stays close to the house the year round. Since I turned seventeen, I've been followin' the big cattle herds up north to make my livin'. I've seen more'n my share of the Chisholm and the Goodnight trails. Never was one to stay in one place too long."

"How old are you?" she asked, after a minute of silence.

He had to think about his answer, counting on his fingers. "If I remember rightly, I'm thirty-one. Never spent much time worryin' about birthdays." He looked over at Jane, trying to guess her age before he asked her. "If it ain't impolite to ask a lady, how old are you?"

She gazed off at the horizon. "I'll be twenty-nine before this Christmas," she said.

"You look younger," he said, which was the truth, in his estimation. "I'd have guessed you closer to twenty."

She smiled. "You're being sweet. I suppose

I'm being honest when I say I've had a hard life, for the most part. When my pa died, I had to grow up in a hurry."

Dan thought about what she'd told him, about going to work at the Crystal Palace. "That's all behind you now," he said, making his voice cheerful. "You can make a fresh start. A drummer told me there's all kinds of opportunity out west, and that's where I'm headed."

She was looking at him when she spoke. "You like a cowboy's life, don't you?"

He shook his head. "Sure do. It's fair to say I'm a respectable cowhand with a rope, an' I like the work. Bein' out in the open on the back of a good horse feels mighty good most of the time. There's a tight spot now and then, but mostly it's a good life. Lonely sometimes, when you get to wishin' you had . . . a girl."

Out of the corner of his eye he saw her smile. "A handsome cowboy like you could find a girl, if you wanted one," she said.

His face reddened. "Most times I'm too bashful to ask a girl if she'll allow me to come courtin' her. Never had much of a way with words around womenfolk. Seems like my tongue gets all tied up in knots."

She didn't say any more, though he could feel her glances now and then, and he wondered why she was looking at him so often.

They rode down the wagon ruts in silence. He scanned the dark landscape for signs of a spring.

Off in the distance, outlined by silvery moonlight, he saw a dark thicket of trees at the bottom of a winding ravine. It was a promising place to look for water and he pointed toward it. "Yonder's a likely spot for a seep spring," he said, "or maybe a catch basin where rainfall collects. Let's get off this road and ride down to have a look."

Swinging south, they trotted across sun-dried summer grass to reach the ravine. The horses' hooves whispered through the grass stalks faintly, the only sound other than the thump of shod animals moving across hard ground.

Dan led the way into the trees cautiously, his hand resting on the butt of his Colt. There, hidden inside the thicket, they found a small pool surrounded by caliche mud. When they rode to the pool so the horses could drink, Dan studied the tracks in the mud. Animals used the waterhole frequently, he judged, but there were no prints left by horses, added proof that he and Jane were alone on the road to Fort Stockton.

Chapter 15

Unaccountably, his fever had returned before morning. The last few hours before daylight were spent clinging resolutely to his saddlehorn, fighting the dizzy spells that came and went. His limbs were trembling with fatigue when dawn slanted across the prairie. Jane noticed the change almost at once.

"Your fever's back," she said, watching him closely. It was a statement, not a question.

"We can't let anything slow us down again," he answered weakly, swaying in the saddle, his knuckles turning white from gripping the saddlehorn to stay astride Buck. "I can make it. We've got to keep movin' till we get to Fort Stockton. By now, Jake's liable to know what happened at the ranch . . . and he'll be comin' hard along our tracks to find you."

Jane's features pinched. "You can't ride in the shape you're in," she said. "We can find some shade where you can rest for a few hours."

He wagged his head. "Keep pushin' west,"

he insisted. "Don't stop — not for anything."
He knew Jake would be behind them, most
likely with Clay and some others to back him.
It was a sure bet that Billy had figured a way
to get free of his ropes by now, and ridden
hard to give Jake the news about Jane. Dan's
fevered sleep had cost them precious time
. . . too much of it. He knew he could tough
it out in the saddle until they reached Fort
Stockton. He just knew he could do it.

He landed hard on his head and shoulder,
and the fall awakened his swollen wound,
sending blinding flashes of fresh pain up his
arm. Dimly, he heard Jane cry out when he
slipped from his saddle. She called his name,
and he heard running footsteps while he stared
blankly at the sky, too numbed by the fall
to move a muscle.

"Dan!" she cried, then he saw her face hovering above him.

His fever had weakened him beyond the
powers of his resolve to stay atop the horse,
and he'd fallen sideways without quite realizing it until he landed. But even now, a voice
inside his head shouted at him that they must
keep moving. "Help me back in my saddle,"
he said, in a voice that didn't sound like his
own, a voice from far away.

Jane's face disappeared. He blinked in the

bright sunlight and tried to think clearly. Then he felt a hand lift his head, and the mouth of the whiskey bottle against his lips.

"Drink some of this," Jane whispered.

He did as he was told, looking up at the woman, at the dark concern on her face. The whiskey tasted bitter, but he took more and tried to sit up, until a trembling weakness defeated his efforts and he gave up, lying in the grass so his strength would return.

Jane shaded his face with his hat brim. "You'll burn up out in this sun," she said quietly, talking to herself. She glanced around them, searching for a tree. "If I can get you over to that mesquite, you'll have some shade. Put your arm around my shoulder, Dan. I'm going to lift you. Lean against me and try to walk beside me. It isn't far to that tree."

He tried to follow her instructions, lifting his good arm to wrap it around her shoulder. He knew he was too weak and dizzy to be of much help, though he struggled to perform the task when he felt Jane lift him uncertainly off the ground.

He managed to get his feet under him. "Now walk, if you can," he heard her say. Thus he commanded his feet to move, though he could not be sure they obeyed properly. Or at all.

Fighting to remain conscious, he experienced the sensation of movement for a time.

When he tried to focus his eyes on what lay before him, he saw only a blur. Then an inky darkness surrounded him and he felt as if he'd tumbled slowly into a black cave.

He awoke in total darkness and felt a blanket around him. When he stirred and swept the cover aside, he felt a hand on his chest.

"Be still," Jane whispered. "Get some rest. Your fever hasn't broken yet. Go back to sleep."

The little voice inside his skull shouted at him to get up and mount his horse. Sensing the urgency in the voice, he tried to sit up and couldn't raise his head. His limbs felt heavy, as though they were weighted down by blacksmith's anvils. "You can't stay with me," he heard himself say. "Jake's coming. Get on your horse and ride for Fort Stockton . . ."

He felt her hand stroke his cheek. "I'm staying with you," she said, "I've a gun and I know how to use it. If Jake shows his face around here before you're able to ride, he's going to end up in a shallow grave. Now go to sleep, Dan, and stop worrying about Jake. I'll make him pay for all those beatings he gave me. I should have done it a long time ago — when I knew he'd never change."

Dan opened his mouth to protest, but something happened to the words he meant to use.

His eyelids closed and he slept.

The ground was moving underneath him. He was sure of it, though his eyes were shut. When he opened his eyes, the world was upside down and he wondered if he might be dreaming. But as consciousness slowly returned, he understood that he was not in the middle of some fevered nightmare. He was hanging upside down across a horse, and the horse was moving.

"Stop!" he cried, knowing his voice was weak, hard to hear.

The horse halted. He glimpsed his injured arm dangling below his head and felt the throbbing pain all the way to his shoulder. Then someone grabbed his waistband and pulled him over the back of the horse. Jane caught him as soon as his feet touched the ground, helping him remain upright until he could steady himself.

"I had to try something," Jane said, watching his face. "I had to try to get you to a doctor, and this was the only way."

He shook his head once and took a deep breath. The sun blazed above him, bringing a question to mind. "How long was I out?" he asked. "I remember falling off my horse . . ."

"You've been out cold more than twenty-four hours, Dan," she replied. "The fever wouldn't break, and now there are red streaks around your wounds. I cleaned them the best I could, but you've got to see a doctor real soon."

Another question popped into his head as he looked down at her. "How'd you get me on my horse?"

She smiled a little. "You don't weigh that much. It took some doing, but I got it done. I rode beside you and held you in the saddle the best I could. I knew your arm would be hurting something awful if you were awake."

His bad arm dangled at his waist without the sling. But when he took stock of his condition, he felt better now. His skin was damp, and the fever had broken. "Hurry and fix that sling again," he said. "I can ride for another spell, I reckon. If I was out cold for a day and a night, you can bet we've got company right behind us. I had it figured for us to have a two- or three-day head start on Jake, but that's all used up. We've got some ridin' to do, and I'll wager we ain't got much time to get it done."

Jane looked down their backtrail, and her eyes clouded. Dan wondered if she could sense how close the danger was behind them, the same feeling that had begun to gnaw away at the back of his brain. Something told him that there was no time to waste.

181

After Jane tied the sling back in place, he lifted a foot tentatively and placed it in a stirrup, gripping the pommel with his good arm. With Jane pushing from behind, Dan made it across his saddle. When she had mounted, they started off at a leisurely pace. Although the ache in his arm remained, he found he was able to ride Buck at a lope a few minutes later without added discomfort.

The road stretched endlessly before them. Dan couldn't guess how far they had ridden, or how far they must travel to reach Fort Stockton. Above their heads, the sun followed them westward. Dan held on to his saddlehorn with renewed determination as the day wore on, for he knew they could ill afford another stop. Jake Logan and some of his handpicked gunmen wouldn't be far behind now. Valuable time had been wasted while Dan lay unconscious.

The sun had become a fiery orange ball in front of them when Dan got his first glimpse of Fort Stockton in the distance. Pale walls of adobe mud and rock arose from the prairie, nestled in a shallow basin surrounded by low, rocky hills. It didn't look like much of a fort, in Dan's estimation, when he saw it clearly. There couldn't be more than a handful of soldiers inside the walls, perhaps a company of cavalry.

Dan let out a whispering sigh when he saw the fort. "We'll be safe now," he said. His fever had not returned during the afternoon and he felt somewhat better.

"Maybe they have a doctor who can look at your arm," Jane said.

Dan kept his doubts to himself. The post was too small and the chances of finding a doctor there seemed unlikely.

Urging their horses to a faster trot in the late-afternoon heat, they started into the basin. Dan looked over his shoulder, as Jane had done all afternoon. The horizon behind them was clear.

"We'll tell the post commander what Jake is up to," Dan said. "There's no telegraph line into Fort Stockton, but maybe he'll send a dispatch to El Paso when we tell him what we know about the cattle rustling."

Jane was frowning. "After we tell the army about Jake, let's keep going . . . as soon as you feel well enough to travel," she said. "Unless the army post has a doctor, we shouldn't stay. You need to have that arm cared for, Dan."

He knew she was right. His arm was more badly swollen than ever, and he'd noticed a milky substance oozing through the bandage that looked yellow in bright sunlight. "I can stay in a saddle," he said, more to reassure her than anything else.

When they reached the bottom of the basin, Dan heeled his horse to a slow lope. Dust arose from their horses' heels as they hurried toward an opening in the low adobe wall. Inside the wall, Dan made out short rows of soldiers' barracks fashioned from caliche mud and stones. By the size of the place, Dan doubted there were more than thirty men stationed here. A slender flagpole stood in the middle of the compound, where the Stars and Stripes fluttered in a dry west wind. Two soldiers guarded the entrance into the fort, and when they saw Dan and Jane, they straightened up from their slouch against the wall to shoulder their rifles, resting the stocks in their palms.

They were waved inside the gate by a soldier. A flat-roofed adobe building sat near the flagpole at the center of the compound, and Dan rode toward it. They drew rein at a hitchrail in front of the building. A burly soldier bearing a sergeant's stripes on his sleeve came through a plank door. Dan eased himself from the saddle and tested his legs before he climbed the steps to the porch where the sergeant stood.

"Howdy, Sergeant," Dan said.

The trooper's eyes were fastened on Jane. "Looks like you folks have made a hard ride," he said, though there was indifference in his voice when he said it, still staring at Jane.

"We've got some important information for the post commander," Dan said, mounting the steps. "We'd like to talk to him right away."

The sergeant shook his head back and forth. "Major Burns is off with a patrol. Renegades hit a ranch in the east part of the Davis Mountains and the major is tracking them. Those renegades took a little white girl prisoner during the raid, and Major Burns won't come back until he finds her, or loses the trail. I'm in charge while the major's away. You can tell me this important information and I'll pass it along to Major Burns as soon as he gets back."

"Do you have a doctor here?" Jane asked, standing beside Dan on the front porch.

The sergeant's eyes flickered up and down Jane's frame. "No ma'am, we don't. This company's too small. Closest doctor will be in El Paso. But we've got a few medical supplies, some laudanum and a few splints for broken bones." He looked at Dan's arm. "Is that arm broken, cowboy?"

Dan shook his head. "It's got a bullet hole in it and the wound's festering some. The slug came through clean, but I've been a mite on the sick side with the fever."

The sergeant shrugged. "I'm Sergeant Hutto," he said. "All I can give you is a few

185

swallows of that laudanum. It kills the pain, but it'll make you drunk as a barn-dance fiddler right after you take a drink."

Dan grinned and stuck out his hand. "I'm Dan Willis, and this lady is Jane Logan. I'd be obliged for the medicine. Rather be drunk than hurtin' so bad. Before I take that potion, I need to tell you about a cattle-rustlin' operation east of here."

The soldier's eyes narrowed. "Cattle rustlers out here?" he asked. "There's hardly any cattle in these parts. Are you sure?"

"Dead sure," Dan answered. "The cattle are stolen up north and driven down to Sutton County to change the brands. Then a feller by the name of Jake Logan drives the herd down to Mexico. It's a big operation. A few days back, they used a running iron on better'n two hundred head before they drove them south."

"Jake Logan," Sergeant Hutto said thoughtfully, like he'd heard the name before. Then he looked squarely at Jane. "Didn't he say your name was Logan, ma'am?"

Jane nodded once. "My husband runs the gang," she replied in a soft voice. "I can tell you enough to put him behind bars for the rest of his life. Jake is also wanted for murder down in Galveston. I saw the reward poster myself. He's a dangerous man, Sergeant

Hutto." She glanced eastward along the road they had followed to the fort. "He's probably close to this army post right now," she continued in a tone that told of her fear. "He'll come after me when he finds out I've run out on him. Jake has to be stopped . . . before he kills anyone else."

The sergeant was clearly befuddled by Jane's story. He gave her a careful examination, then turned to Dan. "Is this the truth?" he asked.

"Saw it for myself," Dan answered. "Watched 'em use that runnin' iron before we left. I was hired on at that ranch to build a fence before I knew anything about the rustling. A word of warning you might give to the major soon as he gets back — Logan's got himself a good-sized bunch of hardcases and gunmen working for him. He won't give up easy. It was one of his men who put that bullet through my arm. I'd wager every last one of 'em is on the run from the law someplace."

Hutto's face darkened. "Come inside, so I can write down the particulars for my report. The laudanum is in the cabinet. I'll let you have all we can spare." He glanced at Jane. "I'll have the cook fix you something to eat, ma'am." He lifted a gloved hand and waved to a soldier across the compound. "One of my men will see to your horses. We've got a good well here, so there's plenty of water for our livestock." He turned for the door and opened it for Jane and Dan. As they walked into the cool interior of the adobe, Dan aimed a look eastward, sensing that someone was coming down the road along their tracks. The feeling was very intense right then, making Dan more certain than ever that he would see Jake Logan again before this business was over.

Chapter 16

The laudanum made him giddy. Resting on a bunk in one of the barracks, he watched the ceiling spin above his head. At times the room tilted drunkenly, and he sat up to put his feet on the floor in an effort to steady his surroundings. In brief lapses in the crazy whirling sensation, he was aware that his wound no longer hurt him. The medicine offered relief, and he was thankful for the small lavender bottle that the sergeant had given him for the ride to El Paso.

It was dark outside the barracks window. Stars sprinkled a velvety black sky. Jane was in the next room, enjoying badly needed sleep. It seemed her troubles with Jake were over now.

Sergeant Hutto had promised that Jake and his men would be arrested if they showed up at the fort. He had listened patiently to Jane's story, jotting down notes with the stub of a pencil in a big ledger on the major's desk.

Dan had added his eyewitness account of the goings-on at the Logan ranch. It was enough, the sergeant said, to warrant Jake's arrest, along with the members of his gang Jane named for the report.

Until Jake had been captured and put behind bars, Dan considered remaining inside the safety of the fort walls. But when Sergeant Hutto saw the angry red streaks leading away from Dan's wounds, as Jane applied a fresh bandage, he warned against any delay reaching the services of a doctor. "Your blood's got poison in it," he said, as though he understood the meaning of the red streaks. "A doctor will have to cut those wounds open or you'll get gangrene and lose that arm."

It was decided that he and Jane would pull out tomorrow for El Paso. The city lay more than a hundred eighty miles to the west, but with the sergeant's warning ringing in Dan's ears, he knew he had no choice in the matter. A one-armed cowboy couldn't handle a rope, or much of anything else. They would encounter the little village of Balmorhea along the way to El Paso, where there was ample water, the sergeant said. But he warned that the road would be empty this time of year, because of dry weather and a growing Indian threat. It was a poor set of choices, in Dan's estimation — run the risk of facing renegade

Indians, or risk losing his left arm — but it hadn't taken long to weigh things. They stood a chance of outriding a band of renegades, but he was powerless in a battle against poisoned blood and gangrene.

Later, he drifted off in a hazy slumber, feeling as if his body were swirling atop the bunk. Without pain for the first time in days, he slept soundly when his slumber deepened.

He dressed in clean clothing, after a small swallow of laudanum allowed him to dress without pain. A smaller dose of the medicine worked almost as well and it did not make him drunk. When he walked out of the barracks into the brilliant morning sun, he looked eastward and thought about Jake again. Even in last night's drunken stupor, Dan had known that Jake wouldn't risk riding up to the fort to ask about his wife, knowing what lay in store for him.

He knocked softly on Jane's door. Soldiers idled about the fort compound behind him. The door opened moments later, and when he saw Jane, dressed in neat riding apparel with her hair freshly brushed, he took a step backward and feigned great surprise. "You're the prettiest sight a man ever expected to see," he said, grinning.

She gave him a warm, wonderful smile.

"You don't look so bad yourself with your whiskers shaved off," she replied.

Free of pain in his elbow, he had taken the time to use his razor at the washbasin in the room. Though his clothing was worn and mended in spots, he figured he looked presentable enough. "That sergeant said we could eat breakfast here," he said. "He swore his cook made good flapjacks, an' they still had a big jug of honey to pour over 'em. I'm starved. Let's walk over and get a bite to eat from Sergeant Hutto and then we'll be on our way."

"How's your arm?" Jane asked, gazing down at the bandage.

"Swelled up like a toad frog in a rainstorm," he answered, "but that medicine is powerful stuff. Can't feel a thing in my elbow just now. Feels like I could ride plumb to California if I took the idea real serious."

She laughed brightly, looking so pretty in the golden dawn sunlight that made her brown hair sparkle and her green eyes flash. He felt good enough right then to notice such things, with the laudanum in his belly. He offered Jane his right arm to lead her away from the barracks. She took it, still smiling, and walked beside him toward the post headquarters.

Sergeant Hutto met them on the porch steps, dressed in a clean blue tunic and trou-

192

sers. He was staring at Jane like a man who'd had a glimpse of the Promised Land, until Dan's greeting distracted his gaze.

"Mornin', Sergeant. We decided to take you up on them flapjacks before we rode out."

Hutto nodded. "Follow me. The cook's been frying bacon since five o'clock and the smell sure has me hungry."

They followed Sergeant Hutto to a long adobe building. Smoke rose in gray curls from a stone chimney atop the flat roof.

With a full canteen, they trotted rested horses out the gate and reined west an hour after breakfast. Dan had made a study of the eastern horizon and saw nothing amiss. By all appearances, they would make it safely to El Paso. Sergeant Hutto said he was sorry he could not send an escort with them, but the ten troopers under his command were needed to guard the fort. As they rode away from Fort Stockton, Dan wanted to believe the worst of their troubles were over, and he did his best to convince himself as Fort Stockton fell away behind them. His pain dulled by laudanum, the arm resting more comfortably now in the sling, he put his mind on the task before them. Reaching Balmorhea required almost two days, according to Hutto, a day and a half if they pushed their horses. Forty miles of rugged road ran between the fort and the settlement.

"I liked Sergeant Hutto," Jane said, holding her chestnut in a rut abreast of Dan.

"I'm grateful to him for the medicine," Dan remarked. "And I figure he'll handle Jake if he shows up at the fort." He looked across the road at Jane. "You're free now. You can go wherever you want and start a new life."

She smiled thoughtfully. "I've been dreaming about this day for a long time, Dan. I feel like a bird that's been let out of a cage."

Dan considered his next words carefully. "Where do you aim to go?"

"I haven't decided yet. El Paso, until you've seen a doctor. Then I might just board a train and head for California, if they have trains in El Paso."

Dan shrugged. "Never been there, so I can't say for sure."

They rode over a hilltop, and now Fort Stockton was out of sight. Dan studied the land in front of them. This country was even more desertlike than Sutton County. Other than the wagon ruts, it bore no signs of civilization. To the north, the land was flat, featureless. Southwest, he could make out the dim shapes of distant peaks against the morning sky.

"We're gonna make it, Jane," he said, taking some satisfaction in his role in it. He had a swollen, busted-up arm to show for the part he'd played, but it was worth it.

They rode into Balmorhea the following day at noon, after a quiet night camp on the prairie. Seated at their campfire, Jane had talked about herself freely . . . the hard times she endured at the Crystal Palace as a frightened young girl, the rough treatment she received at the hands of half-drunk cowboys, her determination to escape that kind of life when she could. Jake's proposal of marriage had seemed like just the right chance to break away, she said. Only much later had she learned that it had been a jump from the frying pan into the fire.

Dan had forgotten all about his injured arm for a while, listening intently to every word Jane said, watching her across the flames. He'd told her about his own upbringing, a life of poverty with few opportunities until he was old enough to strike out on his own. He knew, as he went to sleep long after midnight, that he was falling in love with her, if love was the right word. He found himself filled with strange, wonderful feelings when she was near.

"Not much of a town," he said as they followed the ruts to the eastern edge of tiny

Balmorhea. Scattered adobe huts encircled a sparkling pool of water shaded by cotton-woods and willows. The village was a spot of emerald green in the midst of a dry waste-land. The life-giving water bubbling from the rocks hidden among the trees was a most welcome sight for thirsty travelers.

A single general store sat at the edge of the road running through Balmorhea. Cotton-clad Mexicans of every description lounged around the shaded front porch. Burros and slender mustang ponies rested in the shadows below the trees. It was a peaceful place when they entered it, attracting the stares of the towns-people as they rode to the spring pool to water their thirsty horses.

"Let's stop at the store," Jane said, looking over her shoulder, while the chestnut drank its fill. "I'll buy some tins of tomatoes and peaches, and some sugar for our coffee."

"You'll spoil me," Dan said, grinning. "I'm used to jackrabbit meat and beans. I've got a little money myself. We can share the expenses."

"I'm buying," she answered flatly, as though the matter were settled. Then she looked over at his arm and her face clouded. "The swelling is getting worse, Dan," she added quietly. "I wish there was something I could do . . ."

Dan swung a glance west. "Accordin' to that map, we've got more'n a hundred and fifty miles ahead of us to El Paso. The road crosses the northern edge of the Eagle Mountains. That's where we are liable to run across a few Indians, if our luck runs bad. But we'll make it. I already gave you my word."

She was looking at him differently when he turned his face. He puzzled briefly over the change in her expression.

"I already know your word is good," she said. "If it weren't for your arm . . ."

He tested the feel of it, moving his elbow just a little in the sling. "Long as that laudanum holds out, I'll be okay," he said. "I ain't worried."

They bought a gunnysack full of supplies inside the adobe store and rode away from the hitchrail with tinned peaches, tomatoes, a bag of sugar, and coffee beans. Jane added a bundle of warm Mexican tortillas to their purchases, and as they left Balmorhea behind in a cloud of dust, they ate the round, delicious bread until Dan was sure his shirt buttons would pop.

Camped in a shallow ravine, they boiled coffee and nibbled sweet peach slices from one of the cans, awaiting the contents of Dan's small, smoke-blackened coffeepot. Gazing up now and then at the first stars of the night, they spoke quietly to each other.

"What will you do with yourself, Dan, after we get to El Paso?" Jane asked, studying his face in the firelight.

"Head north when my arm's better," he replied, "up to New Mexico Territory. Hire on with a good cow outfit for the fall roundup. Make a life up there someplace, I reckon."

"I've heard Santa Fe is a pretty town," she said. "I might just go there myself . . . if you didn't have any objections to a woman tagging along."

"No objections at all," he said quickly, feeling a tingle of excitement race through him when he thought about her company. "In fact, I'd like it, if that ain't improper to say to another man's wife. I'd take care of you, till we got there . . . make sure you got there safe."

Her stare lingered on his face. "It's true, Dan, that I'm still Jake's wife. But I haven't loved him for a long time. I don't suppose I ever did. He was my ticket out of Hell's Half Acre a long time ago and I took the chance that things would work out." She paused, and looked into his eyes. "Does it bother you that I'm married to someone?" she asked, speaking in the softest of voices.

He considered his answer before he gave

it, summoning enough nerve to say what was really on his mind. "I know it means there could never be . . . anything between you an' me," he said, and he knew his ears were turning red when he said it.

A slow smile lifted the corners of her mouth. "I didn't know you cared about that," she replied. "I'm a little surprised."

His embarrassment only deepened. "You shouldn't be surprised when a feller is interested in a pretty lady," he told her, with more courage than he knew he had around a woman. "I know it ain't the proper thing to talk about havin' feelings for another man's wife. But I reckon I could have that kind of feeling 'bout you, if you'd allow it." Then he looked down quickly at his folded hands, hoping that he hadn't made a fool of himself.

She gazed at him intently for a long time after that, without saying anything. He squirmed, and busied himself with the tin of peaches, feeling foolish for having revealed his innermost thoughts.

"I might allow it," she said later, whispering. "I'd have to think about it, Dan."

"I understand," he answered back. "We got plenty of time."

She stirred the fire and got up. He found he couldn't look at her right then, too embarrassed by his admission of feelings.

"I'll check on the horses," she said. "Just make sure their hobbles are tight." She walked away from the fire, leaving Dan with a knot in the pit of his stomach that took away his appetite for the peaches.

Chapter 17

The dry land changed as they rode west. Rocky hills became steeper climbs when the road twisted among them. Off to the southwest, mountains loomed. Even the hardy mesquite trees became more widely scattered. Desert brush bearing all manner of thorns held to thin layers of caliche topsoil and grew from crags in the rocks on the hillsides. Since leaving Balmorhea, they had not encountered another set of tracks or seen another living being. It was as if they were the only travelers foolhardy enough to make this journey in late summer.

Just before noon, they halted on a hilltop to rest their horses where a clump of stunted mesquite provided sparse shade. Both geldings were coated with foamy lather in the unyielding heat. Chalky dust layered the horses and riders.

"It's awfully hot," Jane said, wiping her face and neck with a bandana. "I feel sorry for our horses."

Dan swung a lazy look over his shoulder, until his gaze drifted to a spot on the south-eastern horizon where a faint dust cloud lifted into the wind and then bent sharply. "Something's out there," he said, pointing to the dust with his good arm. "Somethin' moving."

Jane squinted at the dust sign. "I see it now," she said, voicing a note of concern.

He watched the dust cloud grow larger; whatever it was, it was coming toward them. "It's comin' our way, whatever it is," he said quietly. They were in renegade Indian country, but the sergeant had also said that an army patrol was out looking for the Indians. "Maybe it's those soldiers Hutto told us about. Major Burns, I think he said, tracking down those redskins who were causing trouble."

"I don't like it, Dan," Jane said darkly. "It could be Jake. Maybe he rode a circle around that army post."

The same notion had wandered through Dan's thoughts. "Let's hope it ain't," he said. His elbow had begun to ache. Thinking about the possibility of gunplay, he reached in his shirt pocket and took out the bottle of laudanum. After he took a half-sized swallow he watched the dust cloud again. On a distant hilltop, maybe a mile to the southeast, he glimpsed four tiny specks beneath the swirling caliche. "Four riders," he said softly, thinking out loud. "It ain't those soldiers."

Jane nudged her horse over and sat beside Dan. "It's Jake," she said hoarsely. "I just know it is."

Dan frowned at the four specks a moment longer. "Too far away to be sure," he answered. "But I don't reckon we can let 'em get close enough to tell for sure. We'd be in rifle range if we did that."

"I'm frightened, Dan," Jane whispered.

He looked at her and noticed how pale she seemed. Or was it only the caliche dust? He watched her pull the .41 from her hip, and saw how white her knuckles were around the gun. "Nothin' to worry about yet," he said, hoping to reassure her. "Not till we know who it is." But even as the words left his mouth, he knew who the four riders would be. Jake Logan had come after his wife, backed by three of his gunmen. Dan turned back to study the dust cloud. He was sure one of the men siding with Jake would be Clay Weeks. "If it's Jake," he added thoughtfully, "we'll fix him a little surprise party." Dan glanced west. "Yonder's a good-sized rock pile on top of that bunch of hills. We can hide our horses in them rocks and have some cover. They get too close, an' I'll trim their whiskers with this Winchester. Come on."

He swung the dun and struck a lope to the

west along the trail, his mind working at a fevered pace. Jane hurried her horse up beside him and when he glanced over at her, he knew she was scared. She clung to the little handgun, watching the riders. "Don't worry, Jane," he said, almost a shout to be heard above the hooves of the running horses. "If that's Jake, he'll be sorry he tested my aim with a rifle."

She stared into his eyes then. "What about your arm? Can you shoot?"

He grinned, trying to calm her fears. "With this medicine in me I hardly feel a thing. Rest easy. I won the turkey shoot back in Possumbelly Flats four years runnin'."

The results of the turkey shoot brought no change to Jane's expression. She turned back in the saddle to watch the dust with her mouth drawn in a grim line. "I'll kill him if I get the chance," she cried, working her palm around the gun. "I won't go back. I'd rather be dead than locked up in that cabin again."

Dan chanced a look over his shoulder. Four men were spread out in an uneven line, their horses galloping toward Dan and Jane. Down in his gut he knew it had to be Jake and some of his gunhands. Only a fool would ride a horse so hard in this miserable heat.

His buckskin was laboring for wind as they began the climb to the jumble of rocks resting between two barren hills. The rocks lay just north of the road by two hundred yards or better. If the four horsemen meant them no harm, they would continue along the El Paso road, missing the rock pile by just under a quarter of a mile. But if the riders swung off the road and made for the rocks, Dan would have proof of their identities. Jake would know that two riders out in the middle of nowhere consisted of his wife and the man who helped her escape. If the four horsemen approached the rocks, Dan was in for the fight of his life.

Their horses galloped up a hillside with air whistling from their muzzles. The rocky outcrop offered protection from the east and south. Reining to ride around from the west, Dan made a disconcerting discovery. The west side of the rock pile lay open. If Jake and his men rushed them from the west, they wouldn't have any cover worth mentioning. A handful of scattered limestone boulders might protect their horses from gunfire. Dan rode hard for the outcrop with a sinking feeling in his belly. The little rock fortress wasn't the best place to make a stand. Yet it was the only form of protection within reach, and with their horses so badly winded it was too big a gamble to try for a better spot farther west.

He led the way into the little rock shelter and swung to the ground, wincing when he used his bad arm. Drawing the Winchester from its boot, he handed Buck's reins to Jane. "Hold onto these horses for all you're worth," he said. "If we wind up on foot, we're as good as dead way out here. No matter what happens, don't let go of those reins. Try to keep out of the line of fire — if there is any."

Jane's face was ghost pale. She was staring into Dan's eyes. "I had this feeling all along," she said softly. "I knew Jake was behind us." She glanced down at her pistol, working her fingers around it. "I swear I'll kill him if he tries to ride up here, Dan. I won't go back."

He forced a grin, hoping to comfort her by sounding sure of himself. "Don't worry. We're gonna be okay."

He whirled away from her and trotted over to the shoulder-high boulders at the southeastern edge of the outcrop. Peering above the rim, he saw the horsemen coming toward them. His stomach did a flip-flop when he made out the riders' faces. Jake Logan galloped his bay at the front of the bunch. To Jake's right, Clay Weeks stared up at the rocks, a rifle resting against his thigh. Flanking Jake on the other side was Billy. And beside Billy, Tom sat his saddle ramrod straight with a Winchester hanging loosely in his right fist. "It's Jake," Dan said over his shoulder. "Billy's with him, and so's that gent Clay

Weeks. Tom's along too, probably itchin' to square things for that time I busted his jaw. Stay down, and hang on to those reins. I'm gonna fire a warning shot in front of 'em. Hope it'll make them think twice about rushing us."

Resting the stock of his rifle atop a rock, Dan sighted in on a spot in front of the running horses, waiting for the right range. As the men drew nearer, Dan thumbed back the hammer and inspected the brass cartridge fitted into the firing chamber. "Gonna be like shootin' turkeys back home," he whispered, sighting down the barrel. It pained him some to grip the rifle with his injured arm, but he held the arm steady and took a bead.

When his finger nudged the trigger, the Winchester exploded with a deafening roar near his ear. The butt plate rammed his shoulder like the kick of a mule as a flash brightened the muzzle.

A spit of dirt kicked up from the caliche in front of Jake's horse. Jake pulled back on his reins and brought his bay to a sliding halt. With the echo of the gunshot still ringing in Dan's ears, an answering shot bellowed from Billy's rifle and a slug went singing off the rocks, barely a yard from Dan's face.

He ducked reflexively while working the lever on the Winchester. An empty shell jacket glanced off the rocks at his feet, sounding like a tiny chime. A fresh cartridge rattled hollowly into the firing chamber, but before Dan could draw a bead on Billy, a gun thundered from the bottom of the hill. A ball of molten lead whistled above Dan's head, sizzling off behind him, harmlessly high. A puff of gunsmoke lifted skyward from Tom's rifle. Then, suddenly, all four horses were moving in different directions. Someone shouted, and Dan was sure he recognized Jake's voice. The men were scattering out to form a rough circle around the outcrop.

Time I took some of 'em out of this fight, he thought. Tom made the closest target as Dan swung his gun sights to the fast-moving shape of a man. Leading slightly with the muzzle to allow for a moving target, Dan gently squeezed the trigger. A single thought raced through his mind as his rifle exploded — he was about to kill a man for the first time in his life.

The Winchester slammed into his shoulder, knocking Dan back a half step with the force of its charge. White light flashed before his eyes, then there was a shrill cry of pain.

Tom was torn sideways from his saddle. He threw his rifle aside, as his hands clawed frantically for his ribcage. Curiously, Tom landed on his feet briefly. He took a few staggering steps forward, tilting more and more while he ran, then he swayed, clutching his side.

Dan watched the affair as though he were in a trance, unable to move when he saw what his bullet had done to the gunman. He paid no attention to the other horsemen galloping away. He couldn't take his eyes off Tom right then, for he knew he was watching a man die. Bitter bile rose in his throat and he swallowed it back, just as Tom's knees sagged. Tom took another halting step, both hands clamped to his ribs, then he crumpled to the ground.

A gun banged to Dan's left, startling him. He remembered the spent cartridge in the firing chamber and levered it out as fast as he could, hardly noticing when the brass tube spun away and fell between his boots. He glimpsed a swirl of gunsmoke as it curled away from the rifle in Billy's hands. Billy spurred relentlessly to get out of range, bent low over his horse's neck, firing over his shoulder. The slug had whined far above the rocks, the result of bad aim taken from the back of a running horse.

Dan sighted in on Billy's back, when a voice cried out inside his skull that he was about to take a coward's shot. Then he reasoned that his circumstances would not allow him to wait for an opportunity that would satisfy his conscience, so he steadied his aim and sent a shot after Billy.

The gun rocked him back on his heels when it discharged, and the rifle's roar muted every other sound around him. But he had hesitated too long and his shot fell short of its mark, kicking up a puff of caliche behind the heels of Billy's horse as it galloped away from the hills.

"Damn," Dan whispered, working the ejection lever again. His conscience had made him miss. Then his gaze fell back on Tom lying facedown in the dirt.

"Dan!" Jane cried. "Jake's coming around this side!"

He wheeled away from the rocks and found Jane pointing to the north. A rider was growing smaller beneath a cloud of dust boiling into the sky, moving in a wide circle to skirt the outcrop, staying well out of rifle range. Dan blinked and shook his head side to side. He cradled the Winchester in the crook of his arm. "He's stayin' wide of us. For now. I shot that owlhoot Tom, but I missed a shot at Billy." He turned his face to the west when he remembered Clay. A lone horseman rode hard away from the rocks. "Yonder he goes," Dan added softly, squinting into the heat haze. "Scattered 'em for a while. They'll think twice before they try to rush us again."

The sound of hoofbeats made him turn around quickly. Tom's horse trotted to a stretch of meager grazing land at the bottom of the hill, then halted, lowering its muzzle to nibble dry grass. The bay was covered with white foam from its ears to its rump. Tom and the others had been pushing their horses hard to catch up to Jane and Dan before they found them.

Dan's eyes drifted back to Tom. Dan let out a ragged breath. He had just killed a man, and in spite of having the best reasons on earth, the idea made him a little bit queasy. He'd been fighting other men most of his life over one thing or another, but never ending things this way. Until now. Looking down at the corpse, he felt older, somehow. And suddenly tired. Something important to the way he felt about himself was gone forever. He was a killer now, in some ways no different than Jake Logan or Billy Cole. Right then, it didn't seem to matter that the man he killed had been trying to kill him.

He heard Jane's footsteps behind him. She halted near his elbow and peeked over the rim to see Tom's body.

"You had to do it, Dan," she said in a quiet voice.

"I reckon" was all he could say. He knew he couldn't describe the way he felt just now.

Chapter 18

Dan and Jane were trapped in a standoff as Jake and his men sat their horses in the distance, watching the rocks from different positions. Billy guarded the road back to Fort Stockton, preventing Dan and Jane from heading back toward the soldiers. Clay Weeks waited near the ruts leading to El Paso, to halt them from continuing west. Jake sat his bay on a knoll north of the outcrop, just beyond rifle range.

After the first hour of waiting Dan's nerves turned raw. "They aim to let us die of thirst," he said.

Jake's plan was easy to figure. One at a time, Jake's bunch could ride off to find water, while the other two kept Dan and Jane pinned down inside the rock fortress until their canteen was empty. Dan knew the plan would work, unless he could figure a way out. "There's just three of 'em," he said. "Leaves one direction open. Soon as it gets dark, we'll make a break for it. South's the only direction they left open for us. We'll have to keep our eyes peeled tonight, to make sure one of 'em hasn't ridden around to the south. There's a chance we'll have to shoot our way through, but it's the only thing we can do."

Jane stirred behind him. "We've got a full canteen. We can wait," she said. "Maybe that patrol led by Major Burns will come along tomorrow, heading back to Fort Stockton."

Dan wagged his head. "Too big a risk. If we wait, our horses will be too weak to carry us at a run if them soldiers don't show up. Without water, our horses are done for in this heat, if we wait."

"I know Jake," she said darkly. "He'll try to set a trap for us. He's making us think the way is clear to the south. It's a trick, Dan. He'll be waiting for us."

"Maybe," Dan said thoughtfully. He looked over his shoulder to the north. "He's sittin' in plain sight yonder, so we'll think he's there after the sun goes down. Maybe north is the direction we oughta ride tonight."

"Don't forget about Clay," Jane warned. "Jake said he was the best shot of any of the men."

Dan thought about his scrape with Billy. "Let's hope his aim isn't much better than Billy's," he said quietly. "If Billy had been any good, I'd be dead. Could be Clay fancies himself a quick-draw artist, but he ain't much of a shot." Then Dan made a study of the road and the hills to the west. "El Paso's the direction we need to ride. My arm's festered, an' I sure don't aim to lose it wanderin' all over west Texas when I oughta be seein' a doctor." He looked toward Jake again, frowning. "It'd be takin' one hell of a chance, ridin' straight for the spot where Jake's sittin' now, after it gets dark. But the more I think on it, the better I like your idea. If we pull out before the moon comes, we'll have the cover of darkness."

"If only those soldiers would come," Jane said wistfully, looking west where the road topped a gentle swell in the prairie.

Dan sighed heavily. "We'll have to handle this ourselves," he said, sounding tired. "That patrol could be a hundred miles from here lookin' for that little girl the Indians took."

He heard Jane's soft footfalls coming up behind him, then he felt her hand on his shoulder. When he turned around, he saw the hardness behind her eyes, the look she wore when she talked about Jake.

"Then we'll ride out tonight like you said," she whispered in a faraway voice. "I suppose I've always known it would come down to this when I tried to get away this time. I'll face whatever comes, just as long as you're beside me."

She reached out and touched his cheek with her fingertips. Her expression softened. She held her hand against his face for a moment and then slowly drew it away.

"We'll be all right," he told her gently. "I bet you'll like it up there around Santa Fe. A drummer told me it was beautiful country . . . pretty mountains with lots of trees and good grass."

She smiled. "I didn't want to go to California, not really," she said. "It was just somewhere to go to start my life over."

Dan swallowed away the dryness in his mouth. "You can start over again where I'm goin'," he told her. "We can both make a fresh start up there . . . and we'd have each other to depend on if things were a little rough right at first. Wouldn't neither one of us be lonely that way."

She moved closer to him, fixing him with a stare, until she was brushing against his chest. Her eyes sparkled with the sun's brilliance and she'd never looked any prettier.

"I'd like that," she said, "having someone like you I could depend on. It seems like I've been all alone for such a long time."

He wanted to kiss her lips right then, even with Jake and his gunmen holding their deadly circle around the rocks. For that brief moment, the danger seemed farther away.

"You'd never be lonely if I was around," he promised. "I'd treat you like a real lady."

Her eyelids narrowed slightly. "My past wouldn't bother you?" she asked.

He shook his head. "Not one bit, it wouldn't," he replied quickly. "It wouldn't matter what you done before. I reckon I've done a few things I wasn't too proud of here an' there, so it'd work out about even."

She stared at him a moment longer before she turned away, and as she walked out of reach, he wished he'd done what he wanted to do and kissed her mouth when he had the chance. It would have been a foolish thing, perhaps, but he'd wanted to do it anyway while she stood so close to him.

He turned back to the rise where Clay rested on his horse and settled against the side of a boulder to wait for nightfall. Riding away from the protection of the rocks would be a dangerous maneuver, but without water for their horses, it was the only move they could make to save the animals. And with Dan's arm festering, he knew he couldn't afford to play a waiting game with Jake Logan because time was on Jake's side.

A buzzard flew overhead, then circled sharply above Tom's body, scenting the blood.

Dan watched the bird until his gaze fell to the corpse. He hadn't wanted to look at Tom again, or think about what he had done. Down deep, he understood that he had to come to terms with himself, especially since he was facing the prospect of having to kill again if they had to fight their way toward freedom.

"It was him or me," he whispered. He told himself that he hadn't had a choice, although he would have much preferred to settle it with fists. Taking another man's life was the last thing he wanted. He'd talked about it easily with Jane, as if putting a bullet in Jake would be an easy remedy to her troubles. When he stared at Tom's body now, he knew he hadn't given much thought to the way he would feel afterward.

It had all seemed so easy when he first talked about it, as though killing men like Jake and his gunhands was akin to swatting flies. Now a dead body lay less than a hundred yards from him, and it was his handiwork. It was an odd time to debate the right and the wrong of it, and he tried to push the question from his mind.

He halted Buck at the edge of the outcrop to scan the dark hills to the north. Without the light from the moon, he couldn't be sure that the hills were empty. But he and Jane had to make their move now, before the moon rose, or they would be seen plainly by the men encircling the rocks.

"It's a gamble," he whispered when Jane stopped her horse near Buck. "A fast-moving target is hard to shoot, so I say we ride as hard as we can and stay low over our horses' necks. If we gamble wrong and ride headlong into Jake or one of the others, it'll boil down to who's the quickest shot and the best marksman. Keep your horse right behind Buck. If there's any shooting, ride as hard as you can for open country. Don't slow down for anything. I'll try to toss some lead at 'em and then catch up. We'll be in a horse race if we can ride through 'em, but I like those odds better than dying of thirst."

He noticed that her pistol was drawn, and he started to object to having her take part in an exchange of gunfire. "I'd feel better if you put that gun away," he said.

"Stop treating me like I'm helpless!" she snapped. "If Jake's waiting for us out there, we'll need every gun we've got!"

Her sudden anger silenced him. He merely shook his head and touched the buckskin's ribs with his spurs. Buck lunged away from the rocks at a bounding run. The horse quickly lengthened its strides, hooves pounding over the dry grass toward the dark hilltop.

He could hear Jane's chestnut behind him, matching Buck's gait across the starlit prairie. Then a distant sound from another direction made him turn his head. Off to the west, a shout echoed. One of Jake's men had spotted them, or heard their galloping horses, and the deadly chase was about to begin in earnest.

"Here they come!" Jane cried.

Dan turned back in the saddle, Jane kept her horse close to Buck's heels the way he'd instructed. When Dan faced front again, he saw the hilltop and drew his .44/.40, thumbing back the hammer without taking his eyes from the direction they rode. The thunder of the horses' hooves drowned out every other sound. For now, the pain in his arm was forgotten as he faced the prospect that a bullet was waiting for him over the top of the rise.

Buck raced up the gentle slope, neck outstretched in an all-out run. The gelding's head bobbed up and down with the power of its strides as it carried him to the crest of the knoll. Dan's heart was pounding as he scanned the darkness. Where was Jake? Were they headed into an ambush when they started down the far side of the hill?

Speeding across the hilltop, the ground suddenly fell away beneath Buck's feet. Beginning the descent so quickly, the horse faltered and slowed over uncertain footing, snorting softly through its muzzle when it entered unfamiliar terrain that was hard to see.

A gunshot blasted to Dan's left, then there was the whine of flying lead in front of him. Dan tried to find the muzzle-flash in the darkness, bringing his pistol up for an answering shot that might slow down the oncoming pursuit. But he saw only inky shadows above the prairie. He couldn't tell where the shot had come from or whether the shooter was close or far away.

The buckskin galloped to the bottom of the hill and stretched its run to top speed across a grassy flat leading north. Dan took some brief comfort in the discovery that Jane had been right about the direction they should ride. Jake and his men were coming after them as hard as their horses could run, but Jane's guess about going north had given them a precious lead. Jane had known her husband well enough to outsmart him, beating him at his own game.

Glancing back, Dan saw the outline of a horse and rider coming behind him; he quickly judged the distance at half a mile. If Buck and the chestnut didn't run afoul of a gopher hole or a rock hidden in the dark grass, Dan knew he and Jane could outride the pursuit before the moon appeared.

His arm had begun to throb. The power

of the buckskin's run had jolted him against the back of his saddle too often and now his swollen wound hurt. A mouthful of laudanum would soothe away the pain, though he dared not risk taking a sip atop the galloping horse, for fear of dropping the little bottle. Gritting his teeth, he made up his mind to endure the ache. It was time to measure his toughness, with so much at stake. He closed his mind to the pain and watched the prairie pass underneath the horse's hooves. Each long stride was carrying him farther and farther away from the likelihood of a bullet, so he forced himself to think about the distance Buck was gaining instead of the fiery pain racing up and down his arm.

He guessed they had ridden almost three miles when he changed directions, swinging westward in a wide arc, allowing his horse to slow. Buck was panting, wind whistling from his muzzle. Dan had made sure that their backtrail was clear before he made the turn and pulled back on the reins.

Jane galloped her chestnut up beside him. They rode shoulder to shoulder for a quarter mile before she spoke.

"I can't see them anymore," she said, looking back.

He, too, glanced over his shoulder and saw empty land. "Your idea was right on the money," he said. "Jake moved someplace else after sundown. That must have been Clay who saw us first and fired that shot. We can aim for El Paso now." He thought about the rough country they were riding. "We'll make better time if we get back on that road. Another mile or so and we'll swing back south and find those wagon ruts where there ain't any gopher holes."

A mile farther west, they angled toward the El Paso road at a slow lope, saving their horses as best they could. Dan wondered what tomorrow might bring, as he and Jane galloped their mounts side by side away from what could have been a far deadlier confrontation. Was it over? Glancing at Jane alongside him, he understood that he was fighting for her future. Their future.

Chapter 19

By the time dawn paled in the east, his neck had grown stiff from looking over his shoulder. Their horses were worn down to a crawl after a nightlong push down the El Paso road. The flesh around Dan's bandage was swollen and discolored, and even with the laudanum in him the pain lingered, dulling his senses.

When he looked at Jane as she rode beside him, her cheeks were sunken and pale. Now that she knew Jake had found her, Dan saw a profound change in her countenance. Tiny crow's feet webbed around her eyes in a perpetual frown. Her fear of Jake was written plainly across her face.

"I'm so sorry I let you get involved in this mess," she said when she found Dan looking at her. She examined his arm with a fleeting glance and her frown only deepened. Then she swung a look backward, squinting into the first rays of morning sunlight. "He's very close now, Dan. I can feel it."

Dan saw nothing against the skyline behind them. "It's just your nerves," he said. "That horizon's clear back yonder." Then, to put her mind at ease, he tickled the buckskin's ribs with a spur rowel and urged the horse to a trot, standing in his stirrups to lessen the jolt of the gait in his swollen arm. Yellow fluid had soaked through the bandage and part of the sling. Time was running short for him to reach a doctor. In his mind's eye, he saw himself with only the stump of a left arm and the vision made him shudder. For what seemed the hundredth time, he turned back to study their backtrail, and found it empty.

A crudely lettered sign hung crookedly atop a slender post at the edge of the road, announcing by way of faded, weather-chipped paint that the name of the unexpected settlement beside the El Paso ruts was Van Horn. Only three bleak buildings occupied the small grove of stunted mesquite trees that shaded the village from the sun's unrelenting heat. Dan guessed the time at three or four in the afternoon as they rode to the outskirts of the settlement, sighting a circle of smooth stones that marked a precious well in the shadows of the mesquite behind the largest of the adobes. A peeling sign across the front of the structure read *Cantina*. A gray mule bearing an ancient McClellan cavalry saddle was tied to a hitchrail in front of the place, swishing flies with its tail. The town looked deserted, if one discounted the presence of the saddled mule. Dan led the way to the hitchrail, where a trough made from crumbling mortar and stones held water for their thirsty horses.

Jane jumped from her saddle and hurried around to help Dan to the ground while the horses buried their muzzles in the water trough. "Your fever's come back," she said, when she saw his face.

He'd been fighting the queasy sensation and dizziness for several hours. He merely shook his head, too weakened to give her a proper answer. He eyed the porch across the front of the adobe cantina. "Help me up to that bench," he said. "I'll be okay after I've rested a minute or two."

She assisted him up two low steps to the cool porch shade, then to a rough-cut wooden bench along the front wall. As he settled on the bench, he let out a sigh and closed his eyes, resting his head on the adobe. "Take care of the horses," he said faintly, slipping away from consciousness. "Tell me if you see anybody comin' down that road. I'm liable to doze off for . . ."

Someone was shaking him, and calling his

name, though the voice seemed to come from far away. His eyelids felt too heavy for him to open them as quickly as he wanted. Finally, he managed mere slits and attempted to focus on his surroundings. For a moment, he wasn't quite sure where he was.

"They're coming, Dan!" he heard Jane cry. She was kneeling in front of him, searching his face. Blinking, he forced his eyes to open fully and then he aimed a look down the two-rut road they had traveled.

At first, three blurred shapes were indistinct in the distance. He sat up and came wide awake in an instant. Jake and his gunmen were headed into the sleepy little town, and soon the silence blanketing Van Horn would come to an end.

"Get our horses around to the back," he said, struggling to his feet. He fingered open his shirt pocket and removed the bottle of laudanum. As soon as the cork popped out of the neck, he took a big swallow of the bitter medicine and handed the bottle to Jane. "Hurry," he said, sighting the three moving shapes, squinting to see them in the heat haze. "Not much time to get ready. Stay out of sight and keep your head down. I'll handle this, if I can."

"Like hell I will," Jane answered quickly, and now that hard look was frozen on her face. "I'll keep them from coming around behind us. Today is Jake Logan's day of reckoning for all those terrible beatings he gave me."

She hurried off the porch to untie the horses before he could object. She led the horses into an alley between the cantina and a smaller building beside it. No one was about in Van Horn, the porches and windows vacant, as though the place were a ghost town. Dan took a cautious step along the cantina porch, testing his legs, to glance through an open doorway. The dark interior of the place looked empty, and he passed the opening to walk to the end of the porch. The three horsemen were less than a quarter mile away now, coming closer at a trot. Dan watched the caliche dust curl away from the horses' heels and rested his right palm atop the butt of his .44/.40. "This is where it ends," he told himself softly, "one way, or another."

He drew his Colt and fingered it, barely noticing that his palm was wet around the grips. Clamping his teeth together, he waited for Jake and Clay and Billy with his heart hammering. In the next few minutes, someone would die and Dan Willis meant to count himself and Jane among the survivors.

The horses trotted closer, until Dan could see the men's faces in the shadows below their drooping hat brims. Jake rode between Clay and Billy. Dan sensed Jake's confidence in the way he sat his saddle for the ride into Van Horn. Jake showed no signs of fear as he rode straight to the edge of town without slowing his horse.

Two hundred yards separated them now, and the three men continued up the street on lathered horses. Sunlight glinted off the pistols they carried in their hands, ready for close-quarters fighting where a rifle would be too slow. Dan watched them approach the cantina as an eerie calm spread through his chest. He wondered if the calm was the result of the laudanum in his belly.

A gust of dry wind fluttered the hat brims of the riders. White dust arose in billowy clouds behind the horses. The sounds of shod hooves echoed across the silence. Dan's thumb went to the hammer of his gun. When he cocked it, the click seemed louder in a strange way, as though some ominous thing magnified the noise as a telltale warning that blood was about to be shed.

Jake suddenly halted his horse in the middle of the road. Billy and Clay stopped alongside him. All three stared at the cantina porch with unwavering eyes. Dan noticed a white cloth bandage around Billy's forehead, partially hidden by the crown of his dust-layered hat.

"You got my woman!" Jake shouted. His voice carried in spite of the wind in his face. "I've come to claim her! You've caused me all the trouble I'm gonna tolerate and I'm gonna kill you, cowboy. You're drawin' your last breath in this dried-up town!"

"Maybe," Dan answered in a loud voice, not a shout, for the wind would help carry his message. "That ain't been decided just yet, Jake. Your wife ain't goin' no place so long as I'm still alive."

Dan saw a crooked grin widen Jake's face. "Me an' these boys are fixin' to remedy that," he said. "You're no match for the likes of us with a gun. You're as good as dead right now, Dan Smith, all on account of a woman who ain't nothin' but a saloon whore!"

Dan's finger tightened around the trigger of his Colt as his temper went on the rise. "She's a lady," he said. "And you're a thief and a murderer, same as them owlhoots who came with you. Your wife stays right here, Jake. Ride any closer, an' I'll prove this ain't just loose talk."

Jake looked over at Clay, then to Billy. "This saddle tramp talks mighty tough," he said, still wearing his lopsided grin. "Let's teach him a lesson, boys. There's an extra fifty dollars to the man who kills him, if I don't get him first."

In the blink of an eye, Jake's gun came up. Dan's right arm was moving in the same instant, swinging up to shoulder level for a well-aimed shot. Dan's finger closed on the trigger when his sights came to rest on Jake's chest, but before Dan's gun exploded in his fist, a gunshot banged from behind the cantina.

All three horses bolted away from the noise of the gun, swaying riders atop their saddles in a moment of confusion. Dan's gun roared and bucked against his palm, just as two guns sounded from the group of gunmen east of the porch. A speeding slug whacked dully into the adobe behind Dan's head, ricocheting off, singing away. Dan flinched and went to a crouch as he sought a fast-moving target among the swirling horses. The riders were partly obscured by the dust from churning hooves as the animals made frantic lunges to flee the rattle of gunfire.

A rider toppled sideways from the back of a charging bay, his hand clawing for his saddlehorn to stop his fall. A gun thundered in the midst of the cloud of caliche. Dan fired at a moving shape in the dust. Above the din from hooves and guns, he heard a voice cry out and saw a shape slumped over the horse's withers as it galloped away to the east.

A gunshot boomed, and a ball of molten lead splintered a porch post just inches from

Dan's chest. Even though the reflex came much too late, Dan jumped away from the post and fired blindly into the dust before he reached the corner of the adobe wall. Above the clump of his boots and the rattle of spurs, he heard Jane's pistol bark at the back of the building.

Now Dan's breath came in short bursts and his chest was tight with fear. His gaze flickered across the road when the dust began to settle. Two riders galloped away from the fight, but one man lay in the road where he'd fallen from his horse. Dan squinted and tried to identify the downed man, covering him with the muzzle of his .44/.40.

The fallen gunman stirred, but his clothing was covered with chalky caliche and Dan couldn't make out who he was. A hat lay in the road beside him, resting on its crown, tilting back and forth like a child's top while it swirled, then wobbled to a stop.

Pounding hoofbeats took his attention away from the road. A horse was moving around to the back of the cantina at a run. Jane would find herself face to face with one of Jake's gunhands unless Dan got there in time. He jumped off the porch to race between the buildings, peering into the shadows below the mesquite around the well. Half blind in the brilliant sunshine, Dan almost missed a dark shape charging among the tree trunks.

A rider bending low over his horse's withers galloped headlong for the back of the cantina. A gun sounded as a finger of yellow flame spat from the rider's pistol. An answering shot banged from a corner of the adobe. Dan knew Jane's life was on the line, facing the full-tilt charge from a spot where there was no protection from flying lead. The clump of his running feet did not prevent him from hearing the crack of a bullet as it struck the adobe wall. Then the rider fired again and the noise blocked out everything else.

The speeding horse bounded out of the trees to an open piece of ground behind the cantina, and when Dan saw the rider's face, he felt a cold chill down his spine. Clay Weeks spurred his horse in Jane's direction with his pistol leveled, steadying the gun for a shot. Running, Dan brought his Colt up and thumbed the hammer back in a single, fluid motion. There was no time to make sure of his target and the shot would depend on luck.

He fired on the run. The sound was like a clap of thunder when the .44/.40 rocked in his hand. Time seemed frozen while Dan watched Clay straighten in the saddle from a violent jolt. Clay's pistol flew from his grip. A shaft of sunlight reflected off the pistol as it flew through the air. Clay's torso fell back across the horse's rump and bounced once when the gelding's back legs struck the ground. Arms flopping at his sides, legs kicking free of the stirrups, Clay rolled off the rump of the charging horse and tumbled toward the earth. He was slammed on his back when his fall ended, and he skidded across the caliche hardpan. His slide sent a plume of dust skyward until his body halted abruptly against a rock.

Dan stumbled to a halt, panting, eyes glued to the body of Clay Weeks. The hard-faced gunman was motionless.

Dan whirled to run back to the road. One more mounted man was still out there somewhere, the man he'd wounded with the lucky shot into the dust cloud. Beyond the cantina, he could hear a running horse somewhere and couldn't make out the direction from which the sound came with so many gunshots ringing in his ears. He ran between the adobes and skidded to a stop when he reached the road. The gunman downed first was still lying in the ruts, but there was no sign of the third man.

Now he could hear the hooves plainly, coming from the south of Van Horn. The horse was hidden behind a squat adobe building on the far side of the road, preventing Dan from judging the direction the horse was running.

Was the sound getting closer?

Gasping for breath, frozen to the spot, a stab of pain went up his injured arm. Then the patter of feet behind him forced him to turn around.

Jane ran toward him, clutching her pistol. He opened his mouth to shout a warning, but the words caught in his throat when he saw her come to a halt, bringing her gun up before her feet stopped moving. For a fraction of a second she seemed to be aiming her gun at him, and the sight numbed him with surprise. "What are . . . ?" His question died on the tip of his tongue just as Jane's revolver thundered.

Wheeling around with Colt leveled, Dan stared into the face of Jake Logan. Jake had gotten up from the ground while Dan's back was turned and now he stood in the wagon ruts with his gun aimed at Dan's belly.

Lightning-fast, Dan cocked his .44/.40 and tightened his finger on the trigger, until something he saw stopped him cold. Blood squirted from a hole in Jake's throat, splattering down his shirtfront. The gun clamped in Jake's fist fell beside his right boot, making a soft thump when it landed. Jake's jaw began to work — he was trying to talk but no words came out, bloody spittle dribbling from his lips. His big hands flew to his neck in an effort to stem the blood. He staggered back, clutching his throat, but his eyes were fixed on Jane. Eyelids slitted with hatred, he slumped to his knees without taking his gaze from his wife. He mumbled a word. "Bitch!" he snarled wetly around the bloody foam bubbling from his mouth.

Dan's trigger finger relaxed. Jake's wound would take his life very quickly. Then a movement distracted Dan. Jane walked past him toward Jake, aiming her pistol in front of her. Dan watched Jane's slow footsteps, puzzled by her approach. She halted a few feet away from her kneeling husband and spread her feet slightly apart.

Jake swayed weakly on trembling knees, staring into Jane's eyes. The cold hate disappeared from his expression, replaced by a look of fear. Blood oozed between the tightly closed fingers gripping his throat. He tried to speak, but there was no sound.

Jane cocked her little revolver and lifted the muzzle to Jake's forehead. "Goodbye, Jake," she said softly, her tiny hands shaking while she steadied the gun.

Dan opened his mouth to shout a protest, but before he could make a sound, Jane lowered the gun and shook her head. Holding the pistol at her side, she turned away from Jake and walked toward Dan on wooden legs with her cheeks as white as snow.

"I couldn't do it," she whispered when she reached Dan's chest. "As much as I've hated him all these years, I just couldn't do it."

Dan glanced across the road, in the direction of the fading hoofbeats. Billy was hightailing it away from Van Horn. The danger was past. Dan holstered his gun and put his good arm around Jane. "It's over, Jane," he said, pulling her close.

A wet groan came from Jake as he toppled over on his face, and the sound startled Jane. Every muscle in her body tensed as she swung a look over her shoulder to the spot where Jake lay in a pool of blood.

"He's dead, isn't he?" she asked in a hoarse whisper.

Suddenly, before Dan could answer, he felt his knees grow weak. The adobe across the road tilted at an odd angle and his vision blurred. He was dimly aware of a sharper pain in his left arm before his eyes closed.

Chapter 20

He awoke to the sensation of movement. Something rattled loudly in his ears. When he opened his eyes, he saw the sky. Puffy white clouds drifted across a bright blue background.

His senses returned slowly. He was lying on his back, and yet he was moving. His mouth had a cottony taste and when he tried to swallow, his throat refused to work.

Where am I? he wondered. How can I be lying down and still be moving? He tried to lift his head and couldn't manage it, as if his skull weighed a hundred pounds. Glancing to either side, he found golden straw around him, bedding straw common to a livery stable. More puzzled than ever, he attempted to reason things out. He was riding in some sort of wagon, a wagon filled with straw.

Then he moved his left arm, and was rewarded by a numbing pain that almost took his breath away. He didn't need to see his arm to know that the festering had gotten much worse. A tight feeling around his elbow kept him from being able to move his arm more than an inch or two. But then, seeing the sky, and the cotton clouds above him, he was silently thankful to be alive.

He wondered where Jane was now, yet he was too weak to raise his head to look for her. He called her name, but his voice was drowned out by the rattle and creak of the wagon. Harness chain clattered somewhere, and an axle protested for want of grease. Now and then, a wheel bumped solidly over a rock, jolting the wagonbed.

He remembered back to the gunfight at Van Horn. A bullet stopped Clay before he could harm Jane, and Billy had ridden off with a hole in him. Jake was dead, and Jane was free of him forever. And it had been her gun that brought him down.

She's one hell of a good shot, he thought, recalling the bullet she fired on the run when Dan's back was turned to Jake. If she hadn't been, he might be stone-cold dead now. He owed her his life.

A thick gray fog swirled around his eyes, threatening to surround him. Through a tangle of hazy, jumbled thoughts, he wanted desperately to talk to Jane, to see her face. But he could not lift his head or summon enough voice to call to her. He was as weak as a new-born kitten and slowly slipping back toward unconsciousness.

He allowed his mind to float toward sleep, painting pictures in his head of tall, tree-studded mountains, and meadows thick with emerald grass. He imagined fat cattle grazing on the mountain slopes and streams of clear water bubbling down the mountainsides. A cowboy rode across a grassy meadow in his vision, and when he could see the cowboy's face, he recognized himself. Riding a sleek buckskin horse that he knew was Buck, he watched himself take a lariat rope from his saddlehorn and begin to build a catch loop near a brindle yearling calf. But there was something about the image that didn't look quite right. And when he looked closer, his mind recoiled at what he saw. The cowboy preparing to rope the yearling had just one arm. A stump filled the other empty shirtsleeve and ended abruptly. The sleeve hung loosely at the cowboy's side.

"Oh no!" he heard himself whisper.

He heard a woman's voice . . . he was sure of it. Strange dreams had haunted his slumber and he did not trust the voice at first. But when he heard it again through the mists of a strange half-sleep, he worked his tongue to shape an answer, although he made no sound he could recognize when he spoke.

"I'm here, Dan," he heard the woman say.

Where am I? he wondered. Why is it so dark here?

He felt himself floating upward, lifted by a gentle wind, and then the mist surrounded him once again and he felt nothing.

The dream returned, gradually taking shape. The one-armed cowboy galloped after a cow across a beautiful mountain meadow thick with wildflowers, attempting to make a loop in his lariat with the use of one hand. He watched himself fail with the effort, and wanted to cry. Over and over again, the cowboy struggled to use the rope while he experienced the sensation of hot tears on his cheeks. He wanted to escape the nightmare, yet some powerful force held him fast to the spot to witness the scene in the meadow.

A scream. A woman's scream came to him through the fog. His eyes flew open when the cry startled him. He found himself staring up at a night sky.

Somewhere close by, he heard the muffled sounds of a struggle, the scrape of moving feet, and the frenzied grunts of a close-quarters fight. His right hand fumbled for his gun, then his fingers closed around it.

Summoning every ounce of strength he had,

he sat up shakily on the bed of straw and turned his head toward the sounds. For a time his eyes would not focus. The darkness was like a black veil.

He discovered that he was in a two-wheeled cart, sitting atop a pile of straw. Crude mesquite stakes comprised a front and two sides around the cart. Beyond the stakes, ten yards away, the low embers of a campfire glowed. And close to the dying fire, he saw two shadowy figures, the struggle he'd heard before he sat up.

His mind cleared suddenly. One of the dark shapes was surely Jane and someone was trying to harm her. Without a guess as to who her attacker might be, he scrambled to his feet in the bed of the cart amid waves of dizzying weakness, and swung his .44/.40 toward the fire.

"Hey!" he cried. A ball of phlegm was stuck in his throat and the warning was garbled, indistinct. His thumb pulled the hammer back as the two figures froze.

"Dan!" Jane's cry for help halted the beat of his heart, but in the darkness, he could not make out which one of the figures was a woman. In the following silence, he heard the unmistakable click of a cocking gun and now he knew he had no choice but to gamble with the life of the woman he loved.

One of the shapes seemed larger in the fraction of a second he allowed himself before his trigger finger pulled. It required only the slightest change in the angle of Dan's gun muzzle to send the bullet where he wanted. With a silent prayer that he had gambled right he squeezed the trigger. An explosion rocked the silence. Dan's heart leaped into his throat.

A grunt followed the gun blast. The larger figure took a step back. Then a groan, a man's groan, was like sweet music to Dan's ears.

He saw the other figure race toward him, and he knew it was Jane, her long hair flying in the wind. He looked back at the man he shot, and saw him stagger over to the firepit, where glowing red coals revealed his features.

Billy's face was a mask of pain. Clutching his stomach, he crumpled to the ground, grimacing, his breath whistling between his clenched teeth. Jane reached the side of the cart before Billy landed on his side. Dan could hear Jane whimpering softly when she ran around to the back of the cart.

Her arms flew around his neck and he dropped his gun in the straw. Salty tears from Jane's cheeks fell on his tongue as she pressed her face against his while he was trying to speak.

"What happened?" he asked. His voice was as shaky as the knees underneath him trying to hold him upright.

"Billy," she sobbed. "He must have been following us. He jumped on top of me when my back was turned. I tried to fight him off so I could get to my gun . . ."

"It's okay now," he whispered. He put his arm around her waist. "I know I got him back at Van Horn. I saw him bend over after I shot him."

Jane drew her face away from Dan's cheek. "His shoulder was bleeding. I felt the blood when I tried to break away. I thought it was over . . ."

Dan looked at the fire, at Billy's face. It's really over now," he said, as more dizziness swirled behind his eyes. "Help me lie down, or I'm afraid I'm gonna fall."

She helped him down on the bed of straw. Her face was very close to his and he could see the sparkle of teardrops in the corners of her eyes. "Don't worry 'bout nothin' else," he whispered hoarsely, eyelids batting to stay awake. "I gave you my promise that everything would be . . ."

He would awaken to the rattle and bang of the cart for brief periods, but no matter how hard he tried, he could not remain awake for very long. It seemed the journey was endless, and in the back of his half-conscious brain, he knew that Jane was taking him through renegade Indian country without anyone's help. If he could rise, he would do whatever he could, but the weakness in his limbs overpowered every effort he made to lift his head or move his legs. Sometimes lying half awake with the sun in his face, he wondered if he might be dying. Hadn't the sergeant back at Fort Stockton said that there was poison in his blood?

I won't die, he thought, filled with resolve to prevent it.

More than ever before in his memory, he had reasons to live a long life. Jane would ride with him to New Mexico Territory, and there was promise of more. She'd said that she might allow feelings to develop between them. More than anything else, Dan wanted that chance, the chance to win Jane's heart.

Dreamless slumber took him under a few moments later. The dream about the one-armed cowboy did not return. Later, he awakened to a mouthful of water and the feel of a cool rag on his forehead. When he opened his eyes, Jane was there, smiling down at him, widening her dazzling green eyes. Wind tossed her soft auburn hair about her pretty face, and the sight brought an involuntary smile to Dan's sun-cracked lips.

"Your fever broke again," she said. "We're

very close to El Paso. A while back, I passed a freight wagon and the man who drove the oxen told me El Paso was about half a day farther. This gray mule can travel all day at a trot, pulling the cart. You're going to be fine, Dan. You'll get to that doctor in time." Her smile grew wider then. "And that's a promise."

He swallowed again when she offered him more water from the canteen. "Sometimes, a man's word is all he's got left," he said. He closed his heavy eyelids and started to drift away on the wings of sleep.

"A woman's word can be just as good," he heard her say, before the fog shrouded his brain, bringing silence.

Chapter 21

Children laughed outside the open window. A gentle breeze fluttered the curtains near his bed. A cloudless blue sky beckoned to him beyond the window frame. . . . He longed to be riding underneath that sky on his way to New Mexico. The sounds of laughter from the children brightened his mood, reminding Dan that he was alive. And that he had two arms. Old Dr. Stokes had said the arm would be as good as new in a few weeks, and he'd promised that Dan would be able to swing a rope or swing a pretty girl around the dance floor if he took the notion.

Dan glanced at the hide-bottomed chair beside the bed. It was empty now, but for what seemed an endless string of days and nights, Jane had sat in that chair and comforted him through the worst of his slow recovery. And as those hours passed, he'd only grown to love her more deeply. He'd been forced to conclude, some days back, that he was hopelessly in love with Jane.

Loving a woman would require some changes in his existence, he knew. Regular baths. Using a razor on his chin most every day, and clean clothes that didn't stink of a man's sweat. Proper manners at the dinner table, eating with his mouth closed and never propping his elbows on the tabletop beside his plate. He'd have to remember to do those thoughtful things his ma always chided him about when he was a boy. It was a strange and wonderful feeling to care for someone other than himself, and he found himself enjoying it more than he ever thought he would.

He heard footsteps on the stairs beyond the door to his room, prompting him to sit up and arrange his hair with a moistened palm. Glancing down at the bandage around his elbow, he took some comfort that the arm was still attached to his shoulder. The dark nightmare about the one-armed cowboy was only a memory.

The door opened a crack, and Dan remembered that Jane had said she was going shopping in El Paso, to pick up a few things they would need for the ride toward Santa Fe. Dr. Stokes had okayed the trip this morning, after an examination of the healing in the wounds.

He saw Jane's bright smile and his heart rose higher in his chest.

"You look like a man who's itching to travel," she said, closing the door behind her, one arm loaded with paper bundles. "I bought you a couple of new shirts and denims, so you would look fit as a fiddle when we get to New Mexico."

A grin tugged Dan's cheeks. "You hadn't oughta done that," he said quietly. "I'll be makin' my own money real soon, so I can buy my own new duds."

She placed her packages at the foot of the bed and came to sit beside him. The look on her face was no longer one of sympathy, as it had been for many days while he recovered from his fever and the dull ache in his arm. "I wanted to buy them for you," she said in a soft, faintly musical voice.

A gale of lighthearted laughter came from the children down in the street. Jane's eyes wandered to the window. "Those kids sound happy," she said.

Dan reached for her hand, and when he touched it, she took her gaze from the window.

"Those kids ain't any happier than I am," he told her. "Knowin' that you're here, I'm as happy as a bear in a beehive full of honey."

Her fingers tightened around his hand, squeezing gently. "I'm happy too, Dan," she whispered. "Happy for the first time since my pa died. It feels good, to be happy for a change. Until I met you, I'd forgotten what it was like."

He raised his head from his feather pillow and propped himself on his good elbow. Then he leaned toward her, and kissed her gently on the lips.

She returned his kiss, and he thought he heard a gentle purr coming from her throat before he drew his mouth away. A warm smile crossed her face as she stared into his eyes. "I think I've fallen in love with you," she said.

Words came tumbling from his mouth, words he never knew he'd be able to say to a woman.

As the afternoon wore on, they talked of many things, revealing more about themselves, their innermost feelings, sometimes saying more with an expression than with words. Jane talked about her past in a faraway voice at times, and it seemed to Dan that she could be talking about events that had happened to someone else.

The sky beyond the window turned crimson with sunset. Jane got up from the edge of the mattress. "I'll go down and get you something to eat," she said. "The doctor says you can start moving around a little tomorrow, now that you're getting your strength back."

Dan's face lit up with anticipation. "Never

was so glad to get out of bed in my life," he said. "I can ride by the end of the week."

Jane turned for the door. "We can take it slow, Dan, when you are ready."

To test his legs, he swung them off the bunk and got slowly to his feet. Dressed only in longjohns, he felt almost naked. "We could leave tomorrow," he said hopefully. "I've got to get up there and sign with a cow outfit before the roundups start."

She smiled. "Speaking of roundups, that Texas Ranger captain told me that he got a wire back from the Del Rio Ranger Post. The Rangers caught the rest of Jake's men and the stolen cattle before they reached the border. He thanked us, for tipping them off, and he said to wire him when we got to Santa Fe. We're entitled to that reward that was posted for Jake down in Galveston. It'll make a good nest egg."

Dan sat back down on the bed. His knees trembled a little when he stood too long. "You're the one who's entitled to that reward," he told her. "It was your fancy shootin' that got Jake."

Her face darkened with the memory of it. "I don't want to think about it," she whispered. "Not ever again. That's a part of my life I want to forget."

Dan shook his head, leaning back against

his pillow. "This can be the last time we ever mention it," he promised. "From here on, we can talk about happier things."

She smiled and blew him a kiss. "I'll be back with your supper," she told him, then left the room.

He listened to her footsteps until the sound faded, with a trace of a smile across his face.

They rode to the edge of a yawning mountain valley. He inhaled a deep breath of clean, cool mountain air, staring at the valley floor. A ranch house was nestled in a clearing beside a wandering stream coursing across the valley. Pole corrals dotted another open stretch north of the ranch house.

"Yonder's home for the winter," he said. "Makin' thirty a month at this job, the sugar bowl will be plumb full of money by the time we see spring."

Jane turned her face from the mountain scenery to look at Dan, silent for a time. "We can be happy here," she said, and he heard the anticipation in her voice.

"It's a small outfit," he added thoughtfully, "but I can handle the chores, even with this stove-up arm. If you can be happy in these mountains, I darn sure can. This is the sort of cowpunchin' job I've been dreamin' about for a long, long time. Won't be no more dust, or long dry spells. It'll be a good life, Jane. And maybe later on, if we save most of that money, we can buy ourselves a little spread of our own."

"I'd like that," she replied. "I won't miss the city life. I had enough of that."

Dan grinned, thinking about what she said. "I never did take to citified ways. Always felt like I was closed in. Out here, I feel right at home. This is where I belong."

She nudged her horse and rode up beside him, until their knees were touching. Buck snorted and rattled his curb chain, tossing his head.

"I belong here too," Jane said softly, looking deeply into his eyes.

He leaned out of his saddle and kissed her. Her lips parted, sending a tingle of excitement through Dan's chest. The feeling was there each time he kissed her.

The bawl of a cow lifted to the rim of the valley. Dan turned toward the sound. "Kinda like music, ain't it?" he asked, watching a longhorn cow trot toward her calf on a slope above the stream.

She laughed. "I suppose it is music to a cowboy's ear," she said. "I wouldn't have called it music . . . not until I met you. A cowboy has different ideas about things, like what makes music."

The bawling ended when the cow reached her calf. Dan watched the calf suckle for a moment. "It's downright peaceful music," he remarked. "I'm gonna enjoy livin' peaceful. It wouldn't be any exaggeration if I claimed I'd had some hard luck for quite a spell, but the way things are right now, I'd say my luck has changed."

Jane tucked her tiny hand in the crook of his arm and stared off at the far side of the valley. "Maybe all our bad luck is behind us," she said.

"Ain't no 'maybe' to it," he replied with a quick, knowing grin. "We'll make our own good luck from here on. You've got my word on that, and you can take —"

"— that promise to the bank!" she cried, finishing it for him as she turned her horse away from the rim.

The employees of THORNDIKE PRESS hope you have enjoyed this Large Print book. All our Large Print titles are designed for easy reading — and they're made to last.

Other Thorndike Large Print books are available at your library, through selected bookstores, or directly from us.

For more information about current and upcoming titles, please call or write, without obligation, to:

THORNDIKE PRESS
P.O. Box 159
Thorndike, Maine 04986

MAY 9 4

RODMAN PUBLIC LIBRARY
215 EAST BROADWAY
ALLIANCE, OH   44601

GAYLORD M